Praise for
Sir Kendrick and the Castle of Bel Lione

"Chuck Black is a master storyteller. The fourteenth-century feel of his books is wholly captivating. *Sir Kendrick and the Castle of Bel Lione* is no exception. Yet the principle anchors of the story—faithfulness, friendship, loyalty, redemption, and forgiveness—are what make it fully worthwhile. Expect to see very little of your young knight after he gets ahold of this book. He will more than likely emerge from the pages with an intensified determination to fight the battles in his own life as a faithful Knight of the Prince."

> —JENEFER IGARASHI, freelance writer, homeschool-resource
> reviewer, and mother of an eleven-year-old Kingdom
> Series fanatic

"Chuck Black has once again transported his readers to the time of knights, castles, and damsels in distress. The Kingdom Series was such an enjoyable read that I was surprised to find *Sir Kendrick and the Castle of Bel Lione* even more delightful… I was drawn into the tale and cared almost immediately for the characters. I rejoiced in each victory, wept with each failing and loss. Chuck is clearly maturing in his skills, and I look forward with great anticipation to his forthcoming works."

> —GAIL BIBY, publications editor for the North Dakota
> Home School Association and author of *North Dakota
> Guide to Home School High School*

"Chuck Black is the John Bunyan for our times! *Sir Kendrick and the Castle of Bel Lione* is a reminder of the origins of the spiritual warfare we are to fight daily."

> —IACI FLANDERS, inductive Bible study teacher and
> homeschool mom

SIR KENDRICK

AND THE CASTLE OF BEL LIONE

THE KNIGHTS OF ARRETHTRAE
BOOK 1

CHUCK BLACK

MULTNOMAH
BOOKS

SIR KENDRICK AND THE CASTLE OF BEL LIONE
PUBLISHED BY MULTNOMAH BOOKS
12265 Oracle Boulevard, Suite 200
Colorado Springs, Colorado 80921
A division of Random House Inc.

All Scripture quotations, unless otherwise indicated, are taken from the New King
James Version®. Copyright © 1982 by Thomas Nelson Inc. Used by permission.
All rights reserved. Scripture quotations marked (KJV) are taken from the King James
Version. Scripture quotations marked (MSG) are taken from The Message by Eugene
H. Peterson. Copyright © 1993, 1994, 1995, 1996, 2000, 2001, 2002. Used by
permission of NavPress Publishing Group. All rights reserved.

The characters and events in this book are fictional, and any resemblance to actual
persons or events is coincidental.

ISBN: 978-1-60142-124-1

Published in the United States by WaterBrook Multnomah, an imprint of The
Doubleday Publishing Group, a division of Random House Inc., New York.

MULTNOMAH is a trademark of Multnomah Books and is registered in the U.S. Patent
and Trademark Office. The colophon is a trademark of Multnomah Books.

Library of Congress Cataloging-in-Publication Data
Black, Chuck.
    Sir Kendrick and the Castle of Bel Lione / Chuck Black ; [illustrations by Marcella
Johnson]. — 1st ed.
        p. cm. — (The knights of Arrethtrae ; bk. 1)
    Summary: Accompanied by the young and inexperienced Sir Duncan, whom he is
mentoring, Sir Kendrick reluctantly sets off to the tournament at Attenbury on an
important mission that holds the future of the kingdom in balance.
    ISBN 978-1-60142-124-1
[1. Good and evil—Fiction. 2. Knights and knighthood—Fiction. 3. Christian life—
Fiction. 4. Allegories.] I. Johnson, Marcella, ill. II. Title.
    PZ7.B528676Si 2008
    [Fic]—dc22

                                                2008005162

Printed in the United States of America
2008—First Edition

10 9 8 7 6 5 4 3 2 1

To my amazing wife, Andrea, and to my wonderful children: Brittney, Reese, Ian, Emily, Abigail, and Keenan. Thank you for the encouragement, advice, and patience, but most of all for your love. May your passion for the Lord consume you!

CONTENTS

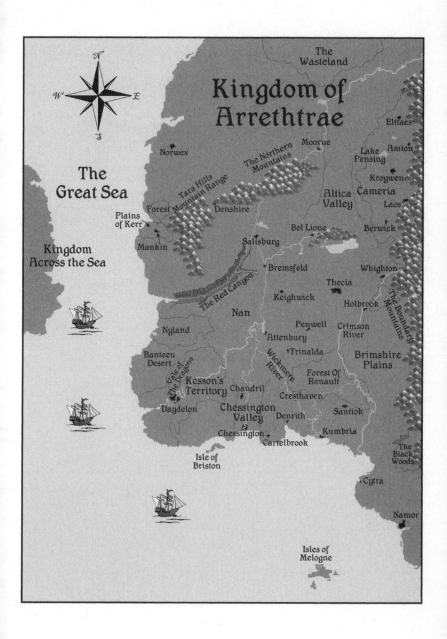

KINGDOM'S HEART

An Introduction to the Knights of Arrethtrae

 Like raindrops on a still summer's eve, the words of a story can oft fall grayly upon the ears of a disinterested soul. I am Cedric of Chessington, humble servant of the Prince, and should my inadequate telling of the tales of these brave knights e'er sound as such, know that it is I who have failed and not the gallant hearts of those of whom I write, for their journeys into darkened lands to save the lives of hopeless people deserve a legacy I could never aspire to pen with appropriate skill. These men and women of princely mettle risked their very lives and endured the pounding of countless battles to deliver the message of hope and life to the far reaches of the kingdom of Arrethtrae…even to those regions over which Lucius, the Dark Knight, had gained complete dominion through the strongholds of his Shadow Warriors.

What is this hope they bring? To tell it requires another story, much of it chronicled upon previous parchments, yet worthy of much retelling.

Listen then, to the tale of a great King who ruled the Kingdom Across the Sea, along with His Son and their gallant and mighty force of Silent

Warriors. A ruler of great power, justice, and mercy, this King sought to establish His rule in the land of Arrethtrae. To this end He chose a pure young man named Peyton and his wife, Dinan, to govern the land.

All was well in Arrethtrae until the rebellion…for there came a time when the King's first and most powerful Silent Warrior, Lucius by name, drew a third of the warriors with him in an attempt to overthrow the Kingdom Across the Sea. A great battle raged in the kingdom until finally the King's forces prevailed. Cast out of the kingdom—and consumed with hatred and revenge—Lucius, known also as the Dark Knight, now brought his rebellion to the land of Arrethtrae, overthrowing Peyton and Dinan and bringing great turmoil to the land.

But the King did not forget His people in Arrethtrae. He established the order of the Noble Knights to protect them until the day they would be delivered from the clutches of the Dark Knight. The great city of Chessington served as a tower of promise and hope in the darkened lands of Arrethtrae.

For many years and through great adversity, the Noble Knights persevered, waiting for the King's promised Deliverer.

Even the noblest of hearts can be corrupted, however, and long waiting can dim the brightest hope. Thus, through the years, the Noble Knights grew selfish and greedy. Worse, they forgot the very nature of their charge. For when the King sent His only Son, the Prince, to prepare His people for battle against Lucius—the Noble Knights knew Him not, nor did they heed His call to arms.

When He rebuked them for their selfish ways, they mocked and disregarded Him. When He began to train a force of commoners—for He was a true master of the sword—they plotted against Him. Then the Noble Knights, claiming to act in the great King's name, captured and killed His very own Son.

What a dark day that was! Lucius and his evil minions—Shadow Warriors—reveled in this apparent victory.

But all was not lost. For when the hope of the kingdom seemed to vanish and the hearts of the humble despaired, the King used the power of the Life Spice to raise His Son from the dead.

This is a mysterious tale, indeed, but a true one. For the Prince was seen by many before He returned to His Father across the Great Sea. And to those who loved and followed Him—myself among them—He left a promise and a charge.

Here then is the promise: the Prince will come again to take all who believe in Him home to the Kingdom Across the Sea.

And this is the charge: those who love Him must travel to the far reaches of the kingdom of Arrethtrae, tell all people of Him and His imminent return, and wage war against Lucius and his Shadow Warriors.

Thus we wait in expectation. And while we wait, we fight against evil and battle to save the souls of many from darkness.

We are the knights who live and die in loyal service to the King and the Prince. Though not perfect in our call to royal duty, we know the power of the Prince resonates in our swords, and the rubble of a thousand strongholds testifies to our strength of heart and soul.

There are many warriors in this land of Arrethtrae, many knights who serve many masters. But the knights of which I write are my brethren, the Knights of the Prince.

They are mighty because they serve a mighty King and His Son.

They are…the Knights of Arrethtrae!

VEIL OF THE MIND

Through the vast realm of Arrethtrae, from the shores of the Great Sea to the Boundary Mountains, from the Wasteland of the north to the lush Chessington Valley, the winds of the kingdom flow across the brows of all people of all stature, the meek and the mighty. And behind the brows of most, even those who would otherwise be considered enlightened, hangs a veil. This veil keeps them from knowing the truth about their land…about their kingdom…about their future.

What is that truth? Simply…that they are not their own. Every day, even whilst they eat and drink and blindly toil for minuscule advances in life, a great war rages around them. It is a war between light and darkness, good and evil—a battle for their very lives—and most do not see it!

One man came to rend the veil of their minds from top to bottom and reveal truth to all who dare look beyond the comfort of ignorance. He was a man of great authority and also great sorrow, for the tearing of the veil cost Him His very life.

It was the Prince who came thus to enlighten the people of Arrethtrae. Those who dare take up His sword and follow Him awaken quickly to a world of war from which one would shudder were it not for the sustaining power of the King and His Son.

Those without the veil of the mind either shrink back or charge forth. For those who choose to move forward into the unseen fray, the stakes appear ever larger, the enemy more formidable, the cause ever more worthy. True courage lies in the heart of one who sees the monstrous form of evil before him but yields not to the fear that calls retreat.

Experience and knowledge give such understanding. Faith in the Prince gives such boldness.

As the winds wander across the regions of the kingdom, they search for those who bear the mark of the King, whose minds are not veiled in darkness, and whose hearts are strong enough to carry the fight of good to the bastions of evil. In the grasslands of Venari, within the city of Trinalda, stand two knights whom the winds linger near, waiting to discover if their story is worthy.

Come, let us join the winds of Arrethtrae and ascertain for ourselves if the saga of Sir Kendrick and Sir Duncan stirs the hearts of men, women, and children to follow the noble Prince!

CHAPTER ONE

A GLINT OF
THE DARK

 The tip of the bright silver blade split the air as it plunged toward Sir Kendrick's chest. But the thrust was ill timed and too committed, considering the advantage Kendrick had over his opponent. Kendrick parried the thrust and countered with a crosscut that threw his opponent into retreat. This seemed to perturb the broad-shouldered young man, who unleashed a wild volley of cuts and slices. Cheers rose from the dozen or so onlookers, each of whom brandished a sword and a look of anticipation.

Kendrick found himself working hard to deflect the young knight's clumsy but powerful blows. A slice came close to striking Kendrick's shoulder, and he fought the urge to counter with the mastery that was available to him. He parried another cut, then held up his left hand and commanded, "Stand down!"

The young man reluctantly lowered his sword.

"You fight with energy and passion, Sir Duncan," Kendrick told him, "but you are reckless in your attack. Be patient and rely upon the skills Sir Augustus has taught you."

The young knight shot Kendrick a look that had little to do with patience. "You were in retreat, sir. I find it difficult to believe you stopped our sparring to tell me that I am too aggressive."

Kendrick stared back at the lad, trying to discern if the comment was a tease or a dare. Tense silence hung in the training arena as everyone waited for Sir Kendrick to respond.

He raised his sword before him as if to invite another fight, but then quickly turned the tip to his scabbard and sheathed it.

"You are correct, young knight. However, it is not the strength of your fight from which I retreat but rather the strength of your, ah…presence." Kendrick put the back side of his hand to his nose as if to filter the air he had to breathe. "I wonder how long it has been since your last bath…"

Laughter erupted around them, and Kendrick quickly slapped the young knight's shoulder as a gesture of reconciliation. The young knight stiffened, then relaxed and joined in the laughter as a burly knight approached.

"That is all for now." Sir Augustus, the training master, waved the young knights to the other side of the arena. "Pair up and practice the moves I taught you earlier. Sir Kendrick and I have business from Chessington to discuss."

He motioned for Kendrick to follow him across the yard, where a water bucket and ladle waited. "It is good to have you with us at the haven."

"You're doing well with the trainees, Gus." Kendrick lifted the ladle of cool water to his lips.

"They're coming along—but what a range of abilities and backgrounds!" Augustus spread his big hands wide. "All they have in common is their devotion to the Prince."

Kendrick nodded. "It has always seemed a little backward to me—first knighting commoners and *then* training them. But then the ways of the Prince always seem contrary to the rest of the kingdom."

"Yes…but the Prince knows what He is doing, even with these lads."

"Are all as reckless as that one?" Kendrick nodded across the yard toward the young knight with whom he'd been sparring.

"Sir Duncan?" Augustus smiled broadly. "Nay, he's the worst."

"Well, you'll have your hands full with him, that's for sure."

"Nay again, Kendrick. You'll have *your* hands full with him." The big knight was laughing now. "He's the one you've come for, the one Chessington's assigned to you."

Kendrick frowned. "I knew I'd regret this trip."

"Ah, cheer up, man. He's a good lad with a strong heart for the Prince." Augustus met Kendrick's eyes. "He's headstrong, true, and perhaps a tad too full of himself. But there's gold in him. Train with him for a couple of weeks, and you'll see what I mean."

Kendrick shook his head. "I've better things to do than play nursemaid to an arrogant upstart."

Augustus laughed again. "I know you, Kendrick. You'll brood and you'll grouse, but you'll also give the lad a chance. You'll be glad of it too." He slapped Kendrick's shoulder. "Come along then. We have some training to do. And it's time for you and young Duncan to get better acquainted."

"Sir Kendrick, I've just learned of a tournament that is to be held soon in Attenbury." Duncan looked hopefully at his mentor as the two rode away from the training camp. After two weeks of sparring together, they had been ordered to report to the Council of Knights in Chessington.

Kendrick merely grunted in reply, so Duncan tried a more direct approach. "I think we should give the tournament a try."

"Why should we do such a thing?"

"Why, to sharpen our skills and improve ourselves as knights. Isn't that the purpose of a tournament?"

"For other knights, yes—and to make a name for themselves. But *our* sole purpose is to advance the kingdom of the Prince and to make a name for *Him*. I find it difficult to believe our participation in such a tournament could accomplish that, and I am quite certain that is not the council's intention for us."

Duncan looked both chided and disappointed, and Kendrick regretted his harsh tone.

"Duncan, I know your heart belongs to the King and the Prince. You are also a young knight who yearns for adventure. But you'll soon learn there is no need. Adventure will surely find you as you follow the course set for you by the Prince." He turned in the saddle to search Duncan's face. "Don't be tempted to ride for glory as other knights do. Such a quest is an empty one."

Duncan nodded glumly as he pondered Kendrick's words. He then turned his head and muttered words that Kendrick could not hear.

Amusement tugged at the corners of Kendrick's mouth. After weeks of training with Duncan, he had grown fonder of the young knight than he ever intended. He admired Duncan's irrepressible enthusiasm and even enjoyed his cheeky charm, though he found it a challenge to redirect the young man's zeal without discouraging him.

Duncan did have potential, though. Augustus was right about that. He was a sturdy, broad-shouldered fellow, and he would grow stronger and mightier in the years ahead if he kept his focus on the Prince and not upon himself. And if he could learn to control himself better—for Duncan's chief weakness was his lack of discipline.

Kendrick assumed this was why the Council of Knights at Chessington had paired the two of them, for Kendrick was a very disciplined knight. Slender yet strong for his build, his demeanor was quite unassuming…until he drew his sword in battle, when all manner of meekness departed and he revealed himself as a warrior of great power. Trying to impart his control and focus to his understudy, however, had so far proved extremely frustrating.

"Let us see what awaits us in Chessington," he said. "Perhaps it will be an adventure more grand than a tournament."

Duncan smiled briefly at Kendrick and raked back his unruly mass of curly black hair. Kendrick smiled back. A full eight years older than Duncan, he had always sought out steadier, quieter companions. Yet he had to admit that being with the lively young man energized him. Perhaps that too was part of the council's plan.

They arrived in Chessington two days later and reported to the council chamber. There was no grand hall or elaborate chamber to host the meetings of the council, only a drafty back room in a boardinghouse.

Duncan looked curiously around him as they walked through the shabby hallway. "I expected something a little more…grand. Do they meet back here to avoid detection by the Noble Knights?"

"The threat of the Noble Knights is diminishing," Kendrick said. "But even still our council has never felt the need to prove themselves with elaborate trappings. The prestige of the Knights of the Prince resides in our cause and not in our dwellings."

The Council of Knights was composed of seven Knights of the Prince. The first knight of the council, who presided over the meetings, was chosen by the other six. He lived in Chessington and served for one year. The other six knights traveled from various cities and regions in the kingdom. Because service on the council usually took them from their homes and families, they served only one year each.

"Greetings, gentlemen," Sir William called out as Kendrick and Duncan entered the council chambers. The two men saluted the first knight and the six other members of the council.

"We are pleased you have made it here in such a timely fashion." A tall, dark-haired knight stepped forward to offer his hand. "I am Sir Jonathan."

Kendrick bowed. "I am honored to meet you."

"Are you acquainted with the rest of the council?" Jonathan motioned to the other six men.

"Some, but not all." Kendrick smiled at two knights he had met on a previous trip.

The nine men exchanged introductions, then took their seats at the large wooden table in the center of the room. After a simple meal of bread and cheese, they turned their attention to the business of the kingdom.

"We have called you here to discuss a matter of great concern," William began. "As you know, for many months after the Prince left us, the Noble Knights brought great persecution to us and were our greatest threat, at least here in Chessington. But as the Knights of the Prince expand throughout the kingdom and the order of the Noble Knights diminishes, a new and more dangerous threat is beginning to be revealed."

Kendrick brought his hand to his chin to stroke his short beard, something he did while focusing intently on a matter. Duncan placed his arms on his knees and leaned forward.

"It is important to remember, gentlemen, that our battle is always with the Dark Knight. Lucius will utilize every opportunity to undo the work of the Prince. Though the power of the Noble Knights appears to be waning, be sure that some other order or guild will rise up to unwittingly do the bidding of this evil warrior." William paused as Kendrick and Duncan pondered his words.

"You say there's a new threat," Duncan said. "What is its nature?"

"We don't know—not exactly," Jonathan replied. "There is always a purpose and an order to the Dark Knight's actions, but such is not always clear in the kingdom as we know it."

Duncan scratched his head. "I don't understand."

Kendrick fixed Duncan with a look that said, *Be patient, lad.* Duncan sighed and nodded as one of the council knights, a stocky man named Channing, reached into his leather belt pouch and removed a silver medallion. He slid it across the table to Kendrick. "Have you ever seen this mark before?"

Kendrick lifted the medallion and studied the engraved image as Duncan leaned near to look upon the piece. It was superbly crafted and would certainly not be found in the possession of a commoner. Kendrick ran his finger across the engraved image, and chills ran up and down his spine. He tried to ignore this unusual response, but the feeling of darkness would not leave him.

The image featured a sinister sword held by a gauntleted hand. Beside the sword was a dragon that seemed suspended above the raised outline of the kingdom of Arrethtrae. Three words were imprinted below: *Ego Mos Vincero.*

"I will conquer," Kendrick whispered.

"What's that you say?" the nearest council knight asked.

"Ego mos vincero." Kendrick spoke more loudly. "It means 'I will conquer.' "

The council knights glanced from one to another with a look of dread.

"I've never seen such a mark before," Kendrick remarked as he handed the medallion to Duncan. "How did you come by it?"

No one on the council seemed eager to answer the question, but Channing finally broke the silence.

"Two of our knights were lodging with a family in a nearby city. After spending the day recruiting and training, they returned to the home." Channing swallowed hard and struggled to continue. "They discovered the parents had been brutally killed and the four children were missing."

Kendrick closed his eyes and felt his heart sink to his stomach. The reality of the fierce battle between good and evil hit him hard. He fought to keep memories of his own past from surfacing

"The medallion was found beneath one of the bodies," Jonathan said. "We don't believe it was left intentionally."

William looked soberly at Kendrick. "I have seen the mark of Lucius on one of his Shadow Warriors; it matches the image of the dragon you see there. We are convinced the medallion is our best clue to the future schemes of Lucius."

Duncan handed the medallion back to Kendrick. Kendrick studied the iconic piece once more and then placed it back on the table, wishing he'd never seen it but knowing he would never forget the image. It felt like pure evil transmuted into a tangible form.

William took a deep breath. "We don't like to dwell on the plots of Lucius, for our mission is simply to take the good news of the Prince to the entire kingdom and recruit as many as are willing. However, we can't ignore or retreat from the attacks of the Dark Knight. That is why we have called you here."

"How can we serve the Prince?" Kendrick asked.

William nodded. "From the reports of fellow knights, we believe Lucius is establishing strongholds throughout the kingdom to train an elite order of knights. We can only guess that his purpose is to bring chaos and discord to the kingdom in an attempt to quell the advance of the Knights of the Prince. We don't know where or who these knights are or even what their methods are, but we are just now beginning to see the results of their efforts."

William picked up the medallion from the table and held it before him. "If this is indeed evidence of things to come, then we must prepare for battle against the fiercest of dragons!"

Kendrick, Duncan, and the council knights all considered William's grave words.

"We need to discover where these strongholds are," said one of the other council members. "And to do that, we must first find the knights they produce."

"The kingdom is vast, gentlemen," Kendrick said. "Can you give us a place to start?"

"There is a tournament in Attenbury not many days from now," William told him. "We want you to travel there and participate."

"A tournament?" Duncan couldn't contain a triumphant grin. Kendrick's brow furrowed.

"My heart is to serve the Prince in any capacity He calls me to," Kendrick said, his voice tight. "But is participation in this tournament truly necessary?"

"There is a suspicion that one of the…ah, shall we say, one of the Vincero Knights will also be a participant. To discover his identity and possibly his origin would be extremely beneficial."

Kendrick wasn't convinced, but he understood he must not let his own reticence hinder his mission. He glanced at Duncan and had the odd compulsion to smack the young man on the head, mostly to wipe the stupid grin from his face.

"I myself would be pleased to participate in the tournament," Duncan offered with a gleam in his eyes. The council knights ignored him.

"Kendrick, we understand your hesitation to return to your former life, but this is not a time to let humility or pain interfere with duty." William glanced uneasily at his fellow council members. "This Vincero Knight will no doubt be very skilled and quite successful in the competition. Your past experience and tournament victories afford us a perfect opportunity to get close to him."

Duncan gawked at Kendrick, his grin transformed into stunned disbelief. Kendrick took a deep breath, hesitated, then let the air quickly escape as he submitted to the council's request. "Do I fight under the banner of the Prince?"

"Not at first," William replied. "Not until you've gained enough information about the mystery knight's identity and possibly his origin. If he's there, of course."

Kendrick pursed his lips together and nodded. "So be it." He stood. "It's off to Attenbury, then."

The other knights also rose.

"The King reigns!" William declared.

"And His Son!" the rest of the knights replied.

The assembly of knights dispersed, and Kendrick and Duncan made their way toward their quarters.

"But when did you—?" Duncan began.

Kendrick held up his hand and shook his head. His mind was already immersed in the mission to come…a mission that left him feeling very unsettled.

CHAPTER TWO

ATTENBURY

The following morning, Kendrick and Duncan rose early and departed for Attenbury. Kendrick noticed Duncan was unusually quiet and caught him glancing toward him from time to time as they rode.

Attenbury was more than a two days' ride from Chessington, but even at a moderate pace, there would be plenty of time before the tournament began to find lodging and stables. That suited Kendrick well. He liked to become familiar with his surroundings and carefully plan his course in all situations.

Kendrick glanced at Duncan and caught his stare once again. "Something troubling you, lad?"

"You…fought in tournaments?"

"Find that difficult to believe, do you?"

"Actually, yes I do," Duncan teased. "Does the Council of Knights have the right Sir Kendrick?"

Kendrick responded with a hard glare and a grunt of annoyance.

"I'm sorry, Kendrick. I mean no disrespect," Duncan hurried to add. "You just don't seem like the tournament type. And what about that speech you gave me about not seeking glory and adventure?"

Kendrick didn't reply, but focused on letting his anger abate. He reminded himself that the lad was ignorant of his past and the pain that lingered there.

"So…" Duncan probed, "were you any good?"

Now Kendrick wished for the silence that had existed before this conversation began. He glanced again at Duncan. "Some may have thought so."

Duncan produced a wide grin and eyes full of impish intent. "I can't wait to see this!"

Kendrick shook his head and turned his attention back to the roadway, wondering if Duncan was more excited about seeing the tournament or witnessing his humiliation.

"Dear Prince," he muttered to himself, "give me the patience."

They camped for the night in a clearing by the roadside. The following morning, Kendrick handed Duncan an unfamiliar-looking tunic.

"Whose mark is this?" Duncan examined the bright red design. "It's not the Prince's."

Kendrick hesitated, lost in thought. "It was my mark before I became a Knight of the Prince." He slipped a similar tunic over his head.

By late afternoon, Kendrick and Duncan arrived in Attenbury. The city already bustled with much tournament activity, and many of the participating knights were arriving. Kendrick and Duncan had no small challenge in finding an inn for themselves and stables for their horses.

The next morning, they walked to the tournament arena, where banners from all across the region fluttered in the breeze. The wealth and prestige of the participating knights was evident by the quantity and quality of their supporting entourages. Kendrick and Duncan found the registry quarters and entered to find two tables set to receive participants.

"Which events will you participate in?" Duncan asked.

"Only the Skill at Arms."

"What?" Duncan looked disappointed. "What's the point in even registering if all you plan to do is the Skill at Arms?"

Kendrick ignored him and stepped forward behind two other knights. Duncan followed him. Just a couple of paces to the right trailed a line of knights waiting to register at the other table. A registrar sat at each table, and a white-haired gentleman, obviously a tournament official, supervised the proceedings.

"I thought you were supposed to be some great tournament knight," Duncan said.

Kendrick slowly turned to face him. He narrowed his eyes and spoke in low tones. "I've never claimed such foolishness. And do not forget that our purpose here is not the tournament!"

Duncan shook his head and looked to the other registry table. He quickly turned back and elbowed Kendrick, nodding toward the knight currently registering at the other table.

"What?" Kendrick asked impatiently. He followed Duncan's gaze and set his eyes upon an imposing knight who wore a tunic of striking azure and gold. Though most knights presented themselves with an air of regal authority, only a few truly possessed the impression without extended effort. Here beside them was one of such caliber.

"Sir Casimir!" The tournament official stepped forward to greet the man. "What an honor to have you participating in our events."

"In which events will you compete, sir?" the seated registrar asked Sir Casimir. "Skill at Arms, Swords, Joust, or all three?"

"All," the knight said tersely.

"Very well, sir. You will obviously be granted exclusion from the qualification runs. The fee is thirty florins, and the Skill at Arms begins in two days. Are there any arrangements that—?"

"Name and origin?" a loud voice asked.

Kendrick broke his focus from the knight at the other table and stepped forward to register. "I'm Kendrick of Penwell."

"In which events do you wish to participate? Skill at Arms, Swords, or Joust?"

Kendrick hesitated just as Duncan stepped forward beside him. He looked toward the knight called Casimir as he turned to leave, and their eyes met. Kendrick felt the man's cold gaze as he peered into the soul of something dark.

He had always been a man of keen discernment, even from his youth. But since he had joined the Prince, his discerning skill had heightened in a way he never expected, especially when he came near to the heart of darkness. He relied upon and trusted this ability, for it had not yet failed him.

The encounter was brief, but it left Kendrick with a feeling of apprehension…and serious resolve.

He turned back to the registrar, who seemed impatient until Kendrick glared at him.

"Ah…your events, sir?" the man prompted.

"All," Kendrick said firmly.

"Very well, sir. Do you have proof of prior participation?" the registrar asked.

"No."

"According to the tournament rules, you must either have proof of prior participation or fulfill the qualification runs before—"

"Sir Kendrick is excluded from the qualification runs." The tournament official stepped up behind their table.

Kendrick and Duncan looked up at the older gentleman. The registrar seemed to hesitate.

"You are Sir Kendrick, also of Bremsfeld, are you not?" the official asked.

Kendrick hesitated. "I am."

The official bowed slightly. "Welcome to our tournament. Please let me know if there are any arrangements you may require me to make for you."

Kendrick nodded his thanks, paid the fee, and left.

Outside the registry quarters, Duncan grabbed Kendrick's arm. "I'm sorry for doubting you, Kendrick. I…I just…" Duncan struggled for words.

"Think nothing of it…it was a long time ago. Or so it seems," Kendrick said. "It's something I wish I could erase from my past."

"But why?"

Kendrick looked at Duncan and then away, into the distance. "It just is. Come, let's get something to eat."

CHAPTER THREE

COLD HEART

The tournament opened with a gala parade and then opening ceremonies that allowed all of the citizens and visitors of Attenbury to join in the spirit of the knightly events and choose their favorites. Kendrick and Duncan rode side by side as the parade slowly made its way through the crowded main thoroughfare. Armor gleamed in the bright sunshine, and banners and tunics waved their colors against a pristine blue autumn sky. Musicians played, and dancers wove gracefully in and out of the procession. Cheers rose from every corner as the procession passed.

Kendrick glanced at Duncan, smiled, and shook his head. The young man seemed entranced by the whole spectacle but especially by the many young maidens who had lined the streets and shops to gaze upon and flirt with the echelon of knights that stretched before and after them. Some honored their favorites by throwing flowers or draping colorful scarves across the horses' necks. Duncan seemed so intoxicated by the attention that he could hardly guide his horse through the crowd.

Oh the foolishness of youth! Was I as full of folly? He smiled again ruefully. *Probably. I just hope the lad grows wiser soon. There's work to be done.*

Qualification runs were held later that day. Since these rounds had been waived for Kendrick, he and Duncan spent the time sparring and then milling about the tents, trying to pick up information that might pertain to their quest. Kendrick especially tried to discover more about Sir Casimir. But they learned little beyond the fact that the man was a tournament regular, he was heartily disliked by servers and merchants, and no one seemed to know exactly where he came from.

"I know he's a Vincero Knight, Kendrick," Duncan said quietly that night as they returned to their quarters. "The way he looked at us…"

"I agree. But we need proof."

"Like a medallion?"

Kendrick nodded. "Like a medallion."

The games opened early the next morning with the first round of the Skill at Arms. All these events were performed with a lance—in full armor, on horseback—and were designed to test speed, agility, and accuracy through various obstacle courses. The knights did not compete face to face but accumulated points based on how quickly and successfully they completed each task. Both Kendrick and Sir Casimir performed well enough in the early rounds to qualify for the finals, where Kendrick prevailed, amassing enough points to win the competition. This meant he would enter the Swords event as the ranking knight.

During the day's closing ceremonies, the top three knights were presented with tournament gold coins indicating their rank in the first phase of the tournament. They stood together on a wooden platform, with Kendrick in the middle, Casimir to his right, and another to his left.

After the presentation, Kendrick turned to offer an arm of congratulation to each knight. But Sir Casimir only sneered and walked away.

Duncan appeared at Kendrick's elbow. "He's a friendly fellow."

"Yes, isn't he though." Kendrick strode off.

Duncan was shorter than Kendrick, and he had to hurry to keep up. "Your performance was amazing! I had no idea…you have a good chance at winning the tournament."

Kendrick tossed his coin to Duncan. "Here's a souvenir for you."

Duncan caught it, his smile fading.

"I won the Skill at Arms for only one reason," Kendrick said, "to make Casimir angry."

"I don't understand you, Kendrick. I don't see how doing well in this tournament could harm our mission or dishonor the Prince. If anything, it's an opportunity to proclaim Him."

"Listen." Kendrick put an arm across Duncan's chest to stop them both. He leaned close to the younger man's ear. "I've been here before, Duncan. Look around you. You may see people full of gaiety and mirth—full of celebration. But all I see are people who are ignorant of the great battle that is waging for their futures."

Duncan's brow furrowed. "But—"

"Don't misunderstand me. I am not against laughter and celebration—or competition, for that matter. But something dark is afoot, and we are here to discover it. Our mission here is not proclamation, but ascertaining the plots of the enemy."

Duncan squinted and nodded. "So tell me, oh somber one, are you as good with the sword as you are with the lance?" Duncan's boyish grin returned.

Kendrick shook his head but couldn't hide his smile. He resumed his walk, leaving Duncan behind to inspect the gold coin.

Duncan quickly caught up. "So why did you want to make Casimir angry?"

"Because angry men make mistakes. In tomorrow's competition I am hoping he will become reckless and reveal some information we need."

"You think he wears the medallion?"

"With the armor, I don't think there is much chance of spotting it. But keep your eyes open. Before this competition is over, we'll no doubt learn what the man is made of."

Unlike the Skill at Arms competition, Swords was a face-to-face event. Each round was timed, and judges gave points for a successful strike or thrust that landed upon the opponent's armor. If a knight lost his sword, suffered injury, or was completely overcome, he was eliminated from the round, and his opponent was granted the victory.

Much to Duncan's delight—and surprise—Kendrick advanced with relative ease. He and Duncan watched Sir Casimir fight each round as well. The man's skill was impressive, and so was his aggressiveness. With each advance, Casimir's tactics seemed to become more brutal.

The crowd swelled as the day progressed. The amphitheater was full for the semifinal round. Kendrick and Duncan watched as Casimir engaged a worthy opponent from Keighwick.

"Casimir's excellent with a sword," Duncan said to Kendrick as they watched the first volley of exchanges.

"He's more than that," Kendrick replied. "He's vicious, and I suspect we haven't yet seen the full extent of his skill or his cruelty. He's holding back even now."

The swords flashed back and forth, and the crowd exclaimed their approval with each engagement. The other knight made an advance and was able to score a wide slice across Casimir's breastplate. The crowd responded with shouts and applause, and the judges scored two points for the knight from Keighwick.

Casimir stepped back as though dazed. His sword lowered slightly, and the other knight came at him with renewed hope. Just when it looked as though Casimir would be scored upon again, he exploded with the power of a battle warrior. The other knight instantly began a defended retreat, but there was no stopping Casimir's furious assault. Within minutes he had scored enough points for a sure victory, but he did not stop. The knight in retreat looked almost helpless as Casimir continued his volley of cuts and slices until he found the perfect opening. He thrust his sword into a shoulder joint of his opponent's armor and angled its path so it would severely injure the knight.

It was a subtle but deadly move, and Kendrick knew it was no accident. The knight collapsed, and Casimir loomed over him like one who had conquered a true enemy. The crowd gasped, and the tournament officials called for aid to be given to the fallen knight.

"Did you see…?" Duncan turned to Kendrick, eyes wide. But Kendrick simply turned without a word and began to prepare for his own semifinal round.

Kendrick's duel was challenging, but he successfully analyzed his opponent's weakness and took advantage of it. The knight never adjusted, and Kendrick ended the round with an easy win. The next contest was the main event of the day—the final round of Swords between Sir Casimir and Sir Kendrick.

"Are you sure you want to do this?" Duncan asked.

Kendrick looked at him and nearly laughed. "I'm the one who didn't want to come here in the first place. Remember?"

"But that last knight, the one from Keighwick—I was told he died." Duncan shook his head in disbelief. "Why would a man be so brutal as to kill another so unnecessarily?"

Kendrick paused and looked at his young charge. "When a man's eye is so full of evil that no good remains within, then evil will do what evil does regardless of the presence of good without. Don't worry, Duncan. I've faced worse."

Duncan stared at Kendrick as though he were reevaluating his opinion of his mentor.

The trumpets sounded, announcing the final round of Swords. Kendrick and Casimir entered the amphitheater amidst uproarious applause. The two knights faced the tournament officials and bowed.

The trumpets blasted once again, and the men turned to face each other. The visors of both knights were still raised, and Kendrick gazed once again into the cold, dark eyes of Sir Casimir. Kendrick knew in his heart that this was no ordinary knight.

The senior tournament official lowered the red and white flag on the stanchion near the platform, and the men dropped their visors. Kendrick took his stance and allowed Casimir to make the first advance. The warrior within him ached to unleash his full potential on Casimir. He had to focus hard to keep the rush of the fight secondary to his mission for the Prince.

Kendrick defended a quick set of cuts and slices, parried a thrust, and countered with a quick combination that nearly scored. The two exchanged offensive and defensive posturing again and again without scoring. Casimir's attacks grew fiercer, and Kendrick found it difficult to defend against the onslaught.

At one point, Casimir sliced from the right and quickly recoiled for a diagonal slice from the opposite side. Kendrick countered both but was unable to bring his sword to bear on the final slice from the left, which found its mark as it cut across his armored chest. Many in the crowd cheered loudly as the judges assessed two points for Casimir. Both men had already worked harder during this duel than in any of the others.

Kendrick stepped back and lifted his visor but still maintained a ready position.

"Your skill with the sword is commendable, Sir Casimir. And your style is unusual. Tell me, sir—under whom did you train?"

Casimir hesitated, but only for a second. Then he advanced on Kendrick with another furious volley that barely left Kendrick time to lower his visor. Defending, Kendrick allowed himself a measure of aggression he had relied upon so successfully in his former life as a tournament champion. His sword flew faster and faster, forcing Casimir into steady retreat and ending with a quick thrust that would have pierced the other man's heart were it not for his breastplate. Casimir fumed as two points were tallied for Kendrick.

Once again the fight paused, and Kendrick lifted his visor. This time, so did Casimir. Kendrick was about to speak, but Casimir beat him to it.

"I've heard of you," Casimir sneered, "and I know who you are."

"Really, sir? And who is that?"

"You are a fool following a fool!" Casimir said with a furious thrust of the sword. The men now fought with their visors up, and Kendrick saw in those eyes the soul of a dark, bloodthirsty warrior.

The crowd at this point was cheering wildly. The bell to end the round brought groans of disappointment, then a collective gasp. Kendrick had relaxed his sword at the sound of the bell, but Casimir, who had just begun a combination, had not. The final slice arced close to Kendrick, and he narrowly escaped losing his head.

The duel ended in a draw. Kendrick stepped back and away and removed his helmet.

"You are an excellent swordsman, Sir Casimir." Kendrick bowed his head politely. "I am honored by your fight."

Casimir whisked off his helmet and stared fiercely at Kendrick, then turned on his heel and stalked away. Kendrick stared thoughtfully after him, then walked to the edge of the arena. Duncan helped him remove his breastplate and spaulders.

"Casimir is a madman!" Duncan said with a scowl on his face. "You are too amicable toward him."

Kendrick smiled. "Yes, like coals of fire on his head. He didn't very much like my friendly overture, did he?"

Duncan considered Kendrick's words and gradually exchanged his scowl for a smile. "Did you learn anything yet?"

"Not just yet," Kendrick replied. "But I'm about to. They're calling us to the ceremony."

Moments later, Kendrick and Casimir mounted the platform, along with Sir Vincent, the knight who had placed third. The crowd cheered as the third-place gold coin was presented to Sir Vincent, then cheered louder as Kendrick and Casimir each received first-place coins.

Kendrick took his coin, held it high above his head to show the crowd, then placed his arm around Casimir's neck. The crowd stood to their feet and applauded riotously. Casimir glared at Kendrick but then reluctantly lifted his coin as well, adding fuel to the cheers of the crowd. Kendrick encouraged Sir Vincent to join them, and Kendrick put his arm around his neck too. The crowd loved it all.

When the applause finally died down, Kendrick slapped the backs of both men and released his embrace. "Well done, gentlemen!" He smiled broadly at them. Sir Vincent smiled in return, but Casimir quickly stalked off the platform.

Kendrick watched him go, then climbed down to where Duncan waited with the horses. The young man's smile was as wide as his face. "You're quite a showman, Sir Kendrick. I had no idea!"

Kendrick hardly broke a smile, but he tossed the second coin to Duncan. The two men mounted their horses and set their course for the inn.

"Is he the one?" Duncan asked.

"I'm not sure." Kendrick turned to look at Duncan. "But I now know he wears a heavy chain about his neck. We just need to find out what it's carrying." Kendrick pursed his lips. "This mission is proving more difficult than I thought. We have but one day left to discover the man's identity and his origin." Kendrick fell into deep thought.

Duncan didn't disturb him. He was preoccupied with thoughts of his own.

CHAPTER FOUR

CLANDESTINE TRUTH

 Duncan stayed awake that night long after Kendrick, who was weary from the day's competition and had fallen asleep quickly. His mentor's steady breathing rumbled through their shared room as Duncan turned over and over on his bed, thinking.

He knew he was fortunate to be involved in such a significant mission. He had only been a Knight of the Prince a short time and had little experience in actual combat. It was truly a privilege to be mentored by a knight of Kendrick's caliber.

But why couldn't Kendrick have more respect for *Duncan's* abilities? The man treated him more like a squire or even a wayward child than a fellow knight. He seemed determined to deny Duncan what he desired most—the opportunity to prove himself.

The dilemma of discovering the true identity of Sir Casimir was just such an opportunity, and Duncan was not about to let it pass by. If he could verify that Sir Casimir was indeed a Vincero Knight and possibly discover the origin of his stronghold, then their mission would be successful and he would have proven himself as a worthy knight.

For the past two days he had been working out a plan to do just that. All he had to do now was wait for the dark of night to fully envelop the town. He turned again in his bed, listening to the night sounds and hoping the plan would work. It was simple but bold and risky.

A lot depended on the girl Duncan had befriended at the inn—a maid named Abbra. A little coaxing and a few coins had proved sufficient to enlist her promise of help. He just hoped she had managed to arrange what he needed.

Finally the occasional barking hound returned to silence. The second hour of the night arrived. It was time.

Duncan rose, fastened a knife to his belt, and quietly exited the room, leaving his sword behind. Careful not to stir a soul, he made his way from the inn to an alleyway behind the Black Crow Tavern nearby. He located a basket and withdrew a long hemp rope.

Duncan smiled. Abbra had done what she promised.

He traveled east through the silent streets of Attenbury, avoiding the occasional drunken forms of recent tavern patrons, until he reached the Crown Inn. According to Abbra, Casimir's room was on the top floor, two windows from the north corner.

He noticed that most of the windows, including Casimir's, were open to draw in the cool night air, for the preceding day had turned unseasonably warm. Duncan's only chance of gaining entrance to Casimir's room was through that window, and getting into Casimir's room was the only way left to find out for sure whether the knight wore a Vincero medallion.

A sliver of moon was Duncan's only light as he made his way to the back side of the inn near the kitchen. This portion of the building was only one story tall, with the chimney for the kitchen ovens jutting up next to the second story. Duncan climbed onto a barrel and hoisted the rope onto the roof. From there he clambered onto the kitchen roof and used the sill and casings of one of the second-story windows, along with the stones of the inn's chimney, to climb to the second-story roof. He fastened the rope around the chimney and carefully made his way along the steeply pitched surface to the place just above Sir Casimir's window.

Duncan paused to catch his breath from the challenging climb. As his breathing grew quiet again, his heart began to race. All of his planning could not prepare him for the intensity of this moment. If he was discovered—and if Sir Casimir was indeed a Vincero Knight—then Duncan's chances of surviving would be very slim.

He had never considered failure and what that would mean not only to him but to the rest of the Knights of the Prince. His muscles tightened and his legs began to quiver as his mind entertained potential calamities. He was quickly losing his nerve.

Stop it! You've come too far to turn back now.

Duncan steeled himself against the encroaching fear, took a deep breath, and slowly lowered himself down the rope to the sill of Casimir's window. The rope was just long enough for Duncan to reach the window, and he was grateful the sill was wide enough to stand on. Using the rope to help him, he was able to balance at the side of the window, listening for any indication that he had been detected. There was none. He quietly opened the window farther and slipped into the room.

Duncan stepped out of the faint moonlight that entered through the window and into the dark shadows of the room. He edged to the left, hoping nothing was there to topple. Then he paused, listening closely to the sounds of deep breathing across the room. He hoped Casimir was as exhausted as Kendrick had seemed to be.

Duncan willed his trembling muscles to relax as his eyes adjusted to the darkness. This room was a fair bit larger than the room at their inn, which was expected since the Crown Inn was nearly twice the cost and reserved for prestigious guests. He scanned the room quickly, hoping he might be fortunate enough to see the medallion on a table or clothes hook. Then he moved across the room, one step at a time, testing each floorboard for creaks before placing his full weight on that foot.

It was a painstakingly long process, but he finally arrived at Casimir's bedstand. He felt the top gingerly with his fingers, searching for the token of evil that would confirm his suspicions about Casimir. His lack of reward forced him to consider the possibility that these Vincero Knights never removed their medallions from their persons.

He felt for the handle of a drawer in the bedstand and gently pulled. It creaked, and Casimir stirred. Duncan froze. Casimir mumbled and rolled toward the edge of the bed nearest Duncan. Duncan slowly moved his hand from the drawer handle to the hilt of the knife on his belt. He waited for Casimir to open his eyes as his mind went wild, considering what might happen next. Much to Duncan's relief, Casimir stilled.

Duncan remained motionless and his muscles began to ache as he waited for Casimir's breathing to become heavy once again. The tension subsided with each passing moment, and Duncan realized he had neither seen nor heard the medallion about Casimir's neck.

Duncan returned his hand to the squeaky wooden drawer and lifted it slightly before pulling slowly once again. With the slides lightened of their burden, Duncan was able to quietly open the drawer far enough to verify that the medallion was not there. He slowly closed the drawer, wondering if he and Kendrick were wrong about Casimir.

He was scanning the room once more, preparing for another trek across the floor, when his eyes came to rest on Casimir's sword. It leaned against the wall, within Casimir's reach. Duncan stepped closer and saw the glint of a chain about the hilt. He reached behind the scabbard and felt the cool metal of a medallion suspended by the silver chain wrapped about the hilt.

Barely breathing, Duncan lifted the medallion out of the dark shadows near the floor. He tilted the sword away from the wall, carefully removed the chain, and returned the sword back to its balancing point on the wall. Careful not to let the chain jingle, he brought the medallion closer to his eyes, adjusting it back and forth until the minuscule amount of ambient moonlight reflected off the image enough for him to inspect it.

The sight of the dragon suspended above Arrethtrae brought chills to his entire body, for the eyes of the dragon seemed to glow and pierce him like fiery darts. In an instant he recognized the presence of evil— and not just one evil knight, but an entire evil force. It was as if this man Casimir was the quintessence of Lucius himself.

Fighting the fear that swelled within him, Duncan forced himself to inspect the medallion further, hoping to find more clues as to Casimir's origin. He flipped it over to see more intricate etchings and a word he did not recognize: *RA*. He turned the medallion over once again and noticed a clearly indented area within the raised map of Arrethtrae, in the central region of the kingdom.

Duncan finished his inspection of the medallion and hung it once more about the hilt of Casimir's sword. As he set the sword carefully back against the wall, he suddenly became overwhelmed with the desire to flee. Handling the medallion unnerved him. So did being in the room with a man whose soul had been darkened by the evil of Lucius and his Shadow Warriors.

Duncan forced himself to move slowly and quietly back to the window. As he lifted himself to the sill, he heard a sound that nearly petrified him. It was subtle and soft at first, then grew with each passing fraction of a moment. The hilt of Casimir's sword was sliding across the wall, leaving its point of imperfect balance. In another fraction of a moment the sword, scabbard, and medallion would crash to the floor, and Casimir would be instantly on his feet.

Duncan thrust himself out of the window and onto the sill as a startled cry and the brilliant crash of steel filled the room with noise that seemed louder than thunder. He reached for the rope and gripped it with one hand as he swung to the side, balancing beside the window with a foot on the edge of the molding.

Duncan heard Casimir's sword slide from the scabbard and looked wildly about him, not knowing what to do. He could never climb the rope to the roof in time to escape Casimir, and jumping to the ground would probably break his legs. He had seen how ruthless Casimir could be in the tournament and knew nothing would stop the man from killing a would-be thief in his own room. He listened to the slow deliberate footsteps approaching the window and imagined a deadly blade preceding them.

Desperate, Duncan readied himself to jump. But then he felt a slight tug on the rope from above. He looked up but saw only the rope bent over the edge of the roofline. Had he imagined the tug?

Hoping against all odds, he reached up and grabbed the rope tightly with both hands. He lifted himself off the sill and then was whisked up and out by a force he could not see.

It happened so quickly that Duncan thought there must be a whole team of men orchestrating his bizarre rescue attempt. He cleared the eave and was set quietly onto the wooden shakes beside a man who seemed as large as a mountain. The rope attached to the chimney was wrapped tightly around one of his muscular arms, and his strong hand held tightly to the portion of rope Duncan was clinging to.

Once Duncan had his balance, the man raised one finger to his lips, and they waited. Duncan heard Casimir at the window below them. After a few moments, he heard footsteps back into the room and the sound of a sword being sheathed.

Duncan took a deep breath and looked up at his rescuer. The man's arms were as big as Duncan's thighs. His jaw was square, his blue eyes penetrating. He said nothing, just gestured with his head toward the place where Duncan had first climbed up.

They moved quietly off the roof and back to the ground. The large fellow strode down the alley away from the Crown Inn. Duncan followed him until the man stopped.

"Thank you," Duncan said, not sure what to expect from this unusual ally. The man was a tower of muscle, and Duncan felt small next to him in more ways than one.

"You know who Casimir is, then?" the man asked in a deep voice.

"Yes," Duncan said. "Who are you?"

The man glared at him. "Tell Sir Kendrick that the battle to come is at Bel Lione." Then he turned to leave.

"What is your name, sir?" Duncan risked the question but expected no answer, and the man offered none. He just turned and disappeared into the night.

Duncan took a few moments to recover from the intensity of the night's events and then made his way back to their inn.

"Bel Lione," he whispered to himself.

How was he going to explain any of this to his mentor?

CHAPTER FIVE

A NEW DESTINY

"You did what?" Kendrick stood paralyzed by anger, his horse half saddled, completely at a loss as to how to deal with the irrational, impetuous actions of his protégé.

"What are you trying to do, Duncan?" He clenched his jaw, trying to stay calm. "Compromise our mission *and* get yourself killed?"

Duncan lifted his chin. "I only did what was necessary to discover the truth about Sir Casimir. And I was successful. How is that being foolish?"

"It was foolish because you did it alone!" Kendrick spoke more loudly than he'd intended. His horse danced away nervously, picking up on the tension, and Kendrick put out a calming hand. "Easy, there, Thunder."

Duncan's countenance dropped, and Kendrick knew his words had hit their mark.

"Duncan, our mission is the same and our efforts must be unified. If you want me to trust and rely on you, then you must not act on your own. Why didn't you talk to me about your plan?"

"I...I guess I thought you would object," Duncan replied.

"Your suspicions of my intent are not enough to risk your life for!" Kendrick took a deep breath. "Next time talk to me before you act."

Duncan looked down to the ground for a moment and then back to Kendrick. "I will. I give you my word."

Kendrick allowed his countenance to soften slightly. "Now…tell me what you learned."

"We were correct. Sir Casimir is indeed a Vincero Knight, for I held his medallion in my hand." Duncan lifted his hand and gazed at the palm as though the silver disk still rested there. "I saw something else. On the back of the medallion was a word I didn't recognize. *RA…* Do you know what it means?"

Kendrick lifted his right hand to his chin. "No, I don't. Perhaps it has something to do with the location where the man was trained."

"Maybe," Duncan said. "But I don't think so."

They both stood in silence as they contemplated Duncan's discovery. Then Kendrick returned to saddling Thunder. "Are you certain Casimir doesn't know you've discovered who he is?"

Duncan didn't reply. Kendrick turned slowly around to face him again. "What happened?" he asked sternly.

Duncan looked sheepish. "Just as I was leaving, Casimir's sword and the medallion fell to the floor. He awoke and investigated, but I was out of sight before he came to the window. He may suspect an intruder, but I'm quite certain he doesn't know it was me."

"Let us hope not." Kendrick reached down to tighten the girth.

"There is one more thing," Duncan said.

Kendrick waited, perturbed at Duncan's piecemeal confession.

"I wasn't alone last night," Duncan added.

"What is that supposed to mean?"

"When I was nearly discovered by Casimir, a large man lifted me to the roof and helped me escape. I don't know who he is or where he came from."

"Did he speak to you at all?" Kendrick asked.

"When we were a safe distance from Casimir's inn, he told me to tell you something—that the battle to come is at Bel Lione."

"Bel Lione," Kendrick murmured.

"Do you know of it?"

"Yes, though I've never actually been there. My home was in that region of the kingdom, south of Bel Lione." He paced a few steps away, then back again. "But how can we possibly trust the word of this stranger? Why would he help us? We don't even know his name."

"True, but he saved me from Casimir."

Kendrick stopped pacing. "We aren't looking for a battle, at least not now. We're looking for Casimir's place of training, and we need more to go on than the cryptic message of a—"

"Kendrick!" Duncan's eyes lit up. "Where is Bel Lione?"

"It is in the center of the kingdom, near a small mountain range. But—"

"That's it! When I was inspecting the medallion, I noticed an indented mark within the outline of the image of the kingdom. It was right in the middle of Arrethtrae."

Kendrick considered this. "I noticed the same thing on the medallion we inspected back in Chessington, but it was in a different region of Arrethtrae. I thought it was just a blemish on the medallion…but what if the indented areas signal different strongholds, different regions of influence for Lucius?"

"The Vincero Knights serve the strongholds?"

"And our friend Sir Casimir may be tied to one at Bel Lione." Kendrick went to his pack and drew out a rolled vellum map of Arrethtrae. He spread it on a nearby bench. "Show me where you saw the indentation on the medallion."

Duncan traced a rough rectangular-shaped region with his finger, and in the center was the city of Bel Lione.

"It looks like your large friend may truly be an ally. Perhaps he is one of the King's Silent Warriors." Kendrick smiled as he saw Duncan's face illuminate with surprise. He put a hand on Duncan's shoulder. "Although I don't condone your method, young knight, I must admit you have gathered enough information to make our mission a success."

Duncan beamed. "So what do we do next?"

Kendrick pondered this for a moment. "Chessington is far to the south, and Bel Lione is even farther to the north. We would lose many days if we first traveled south to report to the Council of Knights." Kendrick rerolled the map and returned it to his pack. "Let us see what lies on the hinder side of those mountains then, shall we?"

"Yes, let's leave for Bel Lione as soon as the tournament is over."

"There is no need to stay for the tournament." Kendrick reached to unfasten the breast collar that helped secure his jousting saddle. "We have what we came for."

"But you are undefeated, and today is the last day," Duncan argued. "If you beat Casimir at the Joust, you could be the tournament champion!"

"We are not here to win a tournament. I participated only to find a knight with a medallion, and your discovery last night has taken care of that. We will leave at once."

"But I am told that jousting is your best event!" Duncan protested. "Surely it could do no harm to finish out the tournament."

Kendrick looked hard at Duncan. "I never planned on being tournament champion, no matter what scenario we faced."

"What do you— You mean you would throw the championship round? Why?"

Kendrick raised an eyebrow, and Duncan shook his head in disbelief.

"Winning this tournament would only draw attention to us, which is something we don't want to happen. But beyond this, when I knelt to become a Knight of the Prince and understood my purpose in His plan, all the accolades of others and the prestige of tournament trophies became pale and worthless to me." Kendrick pointed to the tournament grounds not far away. "This is all silliness when compared to the incredible mission of saving human souls from the clutches of the Dark Knight by the power of the Prince."

Duncan stared at Kendrick, took a deep breath, and nodded. "I understand…I think. But won't your withdrawal bring attention also?"

"You will report to the tournament officials that urgent news from a friend has called me away. That isn't unusual. They will probably deduce that a family member has died."

"As you wish." Duncan left to find the officials.

Kendrick continued preparing Thunder for travel instead of battle, but his mind was already on the road north. What would he and Duncan encounter there?

Sir Casimir was truly a powerful knight and a dangerous adversary. But Kendrick suspected that someone or something far more powerful—and more evil—awaited him and Duncan in the city of Bel Lione.

CHAPTER SIX

THE MYSTIQUE OF BEL LIONE

Kendrick and Duncan traveled north toward a snow-peaked mountain that seemed a hundred-day ride in the distance. Although Mount Quarnell was not the tallest mountain in Arrethtrae, it certainly was one of the most majestic, for it rose dramatically out of the plains and seemed to stretch high enough to pierce the sky itself. A range of smaller foothills clustered around it, and before it lay a beautiful, crystal-clear lake, fed from the crisp streams of the mountain range.

As they neared the mountains three days later, their progress slowed. Bel Lione was nestled in the northern foothills of the range, and it took Kendrick and Duncan another full day just to travel to the opposite side of the range.

They entered Bel Lione late one afternoon and were struck by the beauty of the town. Had they not suspected Bel Lione was a potential source of concern for the Knights of the Prince, they would have thought the whole place had been lifted from the pages of a fairy tale.

A small river flowed from the mountains down through the center of the town, spilling over a number of gentle waterfalls along its way.

The scent of evergreen and wildflowers filled the air. The shops that lined the immaculate streets had been constructed beyond mere functionality; clearly they were intended not only to embrace the beauty of the surroundings but to add to it. Decorative moldings and ornate wooden carvings trimmed the gables, windows, and eaves of all the shops—shoemakers, tailors, barbers, bakers, butchers, taverns, a blacksmith—and most of the homes. The living conditions of the average citizen seemed quite beyond what Kendrick and Duncan were used to seeing in towns of similar size.

In spite of the town's beauty and apparent affluence, Kendrick sensed a slightly forlorn spirit among the people of Bel Lione as he watched them carry on with their work. Had the living conditions been poorer, Kendrick would have thought nothing of it, but the melancholy seemed out of place in such a picturesque setting. He cautioned himself against reading too much into his perceptions. Still, he was sure that something was amiss.

"Where do we start?" Duncan asked as they rode down the cobblestoned thoroughfare.

"Where stories are told that are grand, seldom true, and sometimes based on a few threads of fact," Kendrick replied.

"The tavern."

"Right."

They guided their steeds into the center of town to what looked like one of the largest taverns. As they secured their horses, a cluster of boys a few years younger than Duncan approached. Kendrick found their conversation curious.

"Come on, Brack. You've got to come with us to the festival tonight," one lad said to another.

"That's right," said another. "You're really missin' out."

Kendrick waited as the boys passed by. They didn't seem to notice him.

"I…I can't," came Brack's reply. "My father says it's not right, and—"

"Not right?" The first lad cut him off, and the other three laughed. "What's so wrong about having a little fun?" He slapped the now red-faced boy on the back.

"We'll be by after supper and wait for you outside your window, but we won't wait too…" The conversation faded in the distance.

As Kendrick and Duncan pushed open the tavern doors, the hum of conversation among the patrons dropped to near silence. Since the workday was not yet over, the place was not crowded. A group of elderly men clustered around a window table. Two women leaned over bowls of soup, shopping baskets at their feet. A lone man sat at a corner table, clutching a cup of ale in his right hand but not drinking. His eyes looked hollow and empty.

Kendrick and Duncan found a table, and the tavern owner came to serve them. They ordered something to eat and drink, and the interrupted conversations slowly resumed.

The tavern owner returned, his large serving platter laden with two bowls of dragon-tail soup, a loaf of brown bread, and two cups of ale. Kendrick paid the man.

"What brings ye knights to Bel Lione?" he asked. The man was well kept, as was his establishment. He was middle-aged and husky, nearly bald on top, with the rest of his graying hair tied at the back of his head. He rubbed his hands on his apron, waiting for an answer.

"We're just passing through, but we're quite taken with your town. We thought we might delay our travels a few days. Is there an inn?"

"Several of them, but they're sure to be full for the next few days. The best one is on Lure Road, on the east side of the city."

"I'm sure we'll find it," Kendrick said.

"Can't miss it." He picked up the serving platter and turned to leave. "Just set your course toward the castle."

"Castle?" Duncan said.

The man turned around again. "You haven't seen the lord's castle yet? You must have come in on Tyning Road from the west." He smiled proudly. "Ah, but our castle is a grand one indeed. I thought perhaps it was why you were here." He glanced up. "Uh, excuse me. Customers."

A group of four men had entered. They chose a table not far from Kendrick and Duncan. The tavern owner hurried to take their order while Kendrick and Duncan dipped their spoons into the excellent soup.

"It's festival tonight," said one of the men behind Kendrick.

"I'd give my right arm to be young again," said another.

"Are you lettin' your olders attend?"

"Of course! Why not? They're nearly grown, and this is the time for them to enjoy life a little. Besides, I'm thinkin' one of them might be good enough to become a knight. You?"

"I suppose. I've let her go once already, and I figure she'd just go on the sly, with or without my permission."

"Ain't that the truth," said another, and they all laughed.

"Fools!" came a shout from the corner of the tavern. The voice belonged to the lone man with the cup of ale. "You're feeding your children to the wolves!"

The four men scoffed at him. "Mind your own business, Frayne."

The man stood up and walked over to their table. His eyes were no longer empty but full of anger and pain. "Laugh now, but soon your own won't come back, like my son. Then you'll know!"

"Only the weak ones don't come back," one of the men jeered. The others laughed even harder.

The man named Frayne clenched his jaw, turned, and left the tavern.

Kendrick nodded toward the door. He and Duncan followed the man out of the tavern.

"Frayne," Kendrick called after the man, who was but a few paces away. He turned around, looking puzzled.

"I am Kendrick. This is Duncan. May we talk with you for a moment?"

"Will you mock me as well?"

"No," Kendrick said, "we want to learn from you." They closed the distance to him with just a few steps.

Frayne waited. He was a middle-aged man with a solid frame. Though his physique looked strong and healthy, grief etched his face and made him look old before his time.

"Please tell us what happened to your son," Duncan said.

"Why do you want to know?"

Kendrick looked at Duncan and then back at the man. "We have reason to suspect that Bel Lione may be the source of some disturbing...activity."

Frayne stared at them for a moment. "Come to my shop when you've finished your meal." He pointed to a tailor shop up the way. "We'll talk there."

When Kendrick and Duncan stepped inside the tailor shop a short time later, they were greeted by a voice that matched the feminine beauty of its owner.

"Can I help you gentlemen?" The young woman stood up from a worktable full of fabric. A dress form beside her displayed a partially completed gown, and a variety of shirts, gowns, doublets, and trousers of many different colors and styles hung about the shop. The whole establishment looked prosperous and successful.

The girl looked from Duncan to Kendrick, then back to Duncan. Kendrick smiled to himself. He felt the awkward exchange that happened between Duncan and the lass. He didn't need to look at his young companion to know Duncan was entranced. He couldn't blame his young friend, for the lass was comely indeed.

Her hair was sandy blond and parted to one side. A few tousles partly covered one of her eyes, which sparkled bright blue in the afternoon sun. A warm and gentle smile graced her perfect complexion. The line of her cheekbone was strong. Kendrick was mesmerized for a brief moment, for she bore an uncanny resemblance to his wife. He smiled at her through the ache of his heart.

"Frayne invited us to speak with him. Is he—?"

"I am here." Frayne spoke from a doorway that led to the back room. "Please join me."

Kendrick and Duncan nodded toward the young woman and followed Frayne into a small room stuffed with more fabric, thread, and a plethora of stitching tools. He walked to the center of the crowded workroom, leaned back against a table, and began to stroke his chin in mild agitation.

"Who are you?" he asked.

"We are Knights of the Prince," Kendrick replied, "and we journey here from Chessington."

The man's face registered suspicion and hope. "Why are you interested in what happened to my son?"

"Sir, you can rest assured that we mean you no harm," Duncan said. "We are on a mission to discover the origins of a secret order of knights created to fight against the King and His Son. Our investigation has led us to Bel Lione."

"In the short time that we have been here," Kendrick added, "we've heard of something called the festival."

"I know nothing about a secret order of knights, but I can certainly tell you about the festival." Frayne shook his head. "It's held once a month at the castle, and it's only for the youth of the region. Once lads and lasses turn twenty-one, they are no longer allowed to attend."

"That is quite odd." Kendrick stroked his beard. "What is the purpose of the festival?"

Frayne snorted in disgust. "Lord Ra says it's for them to enjoy life, to—"

"Lord Ra?" Kendrick interrupted. He looked at Duncan and knew that he too had connected the engraving on Casimir's medallion to Frayne's story.

Frayne stopped and looked quizzically at him. "Yes, Lord Ra of the grand castle. He is the one who hosts the festivals as well as a weekly fete. You've not heard of Lord Ra?"

Kendrick ignored the question. "Please go on."

"The festival is a carnival of music, dancing, games, feasts, and frolicking that lasts two full days. And it costs nothing—Lord Ra provides everything."

"Do all of the youth attend?" Duncan asked.

"No, but most do," Frayne said soberly. "My son, Hamlin, started asking to attend when he was fifteen. In my heart I knew it wouldn't be good for him, and my wife was vehemently against it. But all of his friends had attended numerous times. People ridiculed me for denying my son the joy of his youth, and Hamlin kept asking. So I finally relented. I convinced myself that his attending one festival couldn't possibly hurt anything."

Frayne stopped and stared at nothing for a time. Kendrick glanced at Duncan. He wondered if Frayne's story was relevant at all to their mission but decided that anything they could learn about Lord Ra might be helpful in some way. He waited patiently for Frayne to continue.

Frayne finally looked at Kendrick. "Hamlin loved the festival, and at first it didn't seem there would be any problems. But when I said no to the next festival, he left in the middle of the night to join his friends. He also began asking to attend the fetes that Lord Ra hosts every Friday evening. Eventually I wearied of the fight and let Hamlin choose his own path. I was such a fool."

"What happened?"

"I lost my son, that's what happened. Hamlin's whole focus became the pleasures and indulgences Lord Ra offered at the castle. I watched my son begin to wither away from the man I'd hoped he would become.

My wife and I began to fight, and our home became a bed of hostility. I didn't know what was happening. I still don't really."

Frayne's eyes filled with tears. "Six months ago, Hamlin didn't come back from the festival. His friends said they looked for him, but he was gone. They thought he'd left early. I tried to speak with Lord Ra, but…" Frayne's voice trailed off to silence, and he began to gaze into nothingness again.

"Are other boys missing?" Kendrick asked.

Frayne nodded. "Not just boys. Girls too." A fire sparked in his eyes, drying the tears. "It's maddening! Most of them come back week after week, month after month. They're different, but they come back. But some don't come back, and it's as if the city denies that they ever existed. No one will talk about it, and they continue to let their own children march off to Lord Ra's revelry."

"I don't understand," Duncan said. "What does Lord Ra have to gain by hosting a festival every month and fetes every week?"

"He recruits some of the young men and a few young women to become knights that serve in his castle," Frayne said, "and those who are selected fare well indeed. That's what many of the parents are hoping for when they allow their youth to attend the festivities."

"How are they selected?" Kendrick asked.

Frayne shrugged. "I think it has something to do with the games and sports during the festivals, but I don't know for sure. Hamlin wouldn't tell me much about what happened inside the castle walls."

"Tell us more about Lord Ra," Duncan said.

"I don't know much about him really. Just that he is extremely wealthy and, considering the size of his castle, he must be very powerful."

"Can you direct us to his castle?" Kendrick asked.

Frayne laughed. "Certainly…come with me." He exited the back room and walked to the front of his shop. Kendrick and Duncan followed him outside and down the street just a few paces. The main thoroughfare curved to the right and, as they walked, the shops across the street and the trees behind them slowly retreated from view to reveal a magnificent castle set against the beautiful green of the forest and the rocky backdrop of Mount Quarnell. For all the castle's beauty and splendor, however, Kendrick felt the hairs on his neck stand straight, for he felt the powerful shadow of great evil lurking behind the massive walls.

Kendrick laid a hand on his companion's shoulder. "Well, Duncan, something tells me we've found what we've been looking for."

Duncan nodded. "I believe you're right. But how do we find out for sure?"

"We'll have to stay for a while and do some investigating." Kendrick broke his gaze from the castle of Bel Lione and looked at Frayne. "I'm told there is an inn over on Lure Road. Is it a good place to stay?"

"It is, but I doubt you'll find any rooms available," Frayne said. "Not with the festival this week. Although it is just for the youth, the activity brings many travelers from all across the region. Parents bring their children to attend and their wares to sell. In fact, I'm afraid all the inns will be full by now. You could try—"

"Excuse me," a soft voice said from behind. "My mother sometimes boards visitors, and we have a couple of empty rooms available."

The three men turned to see that Frayne's tailor maid had followed them the few paces from his shop.

Kendrick was puzzled. "I thought she was your daughter," he said to Frayne.

"No, Elise is not my daughter. But she brightens my shop—and my heart—as though she were." Frayne smiled and put his hand out to the young woman, who took his hand and moved to stand next to him. "Forgive me for not introducing you earlier. Sir Kendrick, Sir Duncan… please meet Maid Elise of Lionsgate, daughter of Lady Odette."

Both knights bowed and Maid Elise curtsied with grace. Frayne lightly placed a hand upon her shoulder. "Elise and I have something in common. We have both lost someone very dear to us—I my son, and she her father—perhaps to the same villain."

Elise's eyes momentarily lost their sparkle as she looked to the ground and then back to the men. "I work for Frayne when Mother doesn't need me at the manor. With Father gone, we must look for other means to provide for ourselves."

"Are you sure you would have room for us?" Duncan asked.

"Oh yes." Her smile returned. "Our home is quite large, and it is just my brother and me at home with Mother now."

"Why don't you take them to Lady Odette, Elise," Frayne said. "I can manage the shop for the rest of the day."

Elise placed a hand on top of his and looked up at him.

"I'm all right now...really," he said.

She nodded. "I'll be just a moment, gentlemen." With that she turned and went back into the shop. Duncan watched her all the while.

Kendrick turned to Frayne. "Thank you for your help. For what it's worth, we believe you. There is much more happening here than a monthly celebration for the city's youth."

"May we come and visit with you again?" Duncan asked. "I'm sure there are some elements of your story that will make more sense to us as we learn more about Lord Ra."

"Yes...of course." The man looked as though some of his burden had been lifted. "Please come anytime."

CHAPTER SEVEN

A COUNTRY MANOR

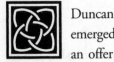Duncan and Kendrick arrived back at the shop just as Elise emerged carrying a small satchel. Duncan stammered out an offer for Elise to ride his horse, and she graciously accepted. She guided them down various streets toward the southwestern edge of the city, then pointed out a road that led into the country.

"It's not far now," she said. "We live a short distance out of Bel Lione."

Before they had gone far, Elise directed them down a less-traveled road that branched off to the right. Large trees stretched their limbs overhead to form a shady tunnel, now vibrant with colorful autumn leaves. Duncan, who had been tongue-tied since he met Elise, gradually relaxed as they went down this enchanted byway, and soon the two young people were engaged in small talk. Kendrick lingered slightly behind them, wondering if Duncan had any inkling as to how to win a maiden's heart.

The end of the road brought them to the beautiful front courtyard of a rambling, unpretentious manor house. The place looked comfortable and inviting, although ragged hedges and worn paint gave evidence the estate had fallen on difficult times. Kendrick assumed the death of Elise's father had something to do with that.

A boy of about sixteen came to greet them as they neared the manor.

"Hello, Ancel," Elise said as she dismounted.

"Hi, El," he said with a look of curiosity on his face. He was a handsome youth whose blond hair was darker and curlier than Elise's.

"Sir Kendrick, Sir Duncan, I would like you to meet my brother, Ancel. Ancel, these gentlemen are looking for room and board for a few weeks."

"You're knights, aren't you?" Ancel blurted out, his eyes shining. "My father was a knight. I'm going to be one someday!"

"Then we should talk," Kendrick answered with a smile.

"What order do you belong to?" Ancel asked.

"We are Knights of the Prince," Duncan replied, "and we're on a mission of discovery."

"Really?" the boy asked with a quizzical gaze. "What's there to discover in Bel Lione?"

"Ancel!" Elise said with a tone of mild rebuke. "These gentlemen are tired from their journey. Please take their horses to the stable and see that they are well cared for."

Ancel's smile returned. "Sure, El."

"Is Mother about?" she asked.

"I think she's in the kitchen." Ancel reached for Thunder's reins. "If you catch her, she may have time to put on some extra food for dinner."

Elise led Duncan and Kendrick into the manor, seated them in a comfortable parlor, and excused herself. She returned with a stately looking woman that Kendrick presumed was Lady Odette. The resemblance between Elise and her mother was obvious.

"Good afternoon, gentlemen. I am Lady Odette of Lionsgate."

Kendrick and Duncan rose and bowed. "It is a pleasure to meet you. I am Kendrick of Penwell, and this is Duncan of Trinalda."

"Elise tells me you are in need of room and board."

"Yes, my lady, if it isn't too much of an inconvenience."

"Not at all. We often host gentry from other cities when the inns are full." Lady Odette smiled apologetically. "I hope you will forgive the rudimentary service. My two children and I have had to take on the duties of our former servants. Our situation has become a bit difficult since my husband passed away."

"We are grateful for a bed," Kendrick replied, "and expect nothing else."

She smiled. "If your business allows, we should be delighted to have you join us for our meals—midmorning and late afternoon. Just let me know the evening before."

"We would be honored," Kendrick said.

"Elise, please take them to the guest rooms while I finish preparing the meal."

Kendrick and Duncan remained at Lionsgate for many days, learning as much as they could about the castle at Bel Lione. They were careful not to draw too much attention to themselves, for if Kendrick's suspicions were true, Lord Ra would not ignore their investigation. The town of Bel Lione was large enough to hide their identities, at least for a time, and staying beyond the town's edge at Lady Odette's manor helped greatly.

Duncan took it upon himself to escort Elise to the tailor's shop each morning, and Kendrick suspected his young friend was stricken with love. Over the passing weeks, it became obvious that Elise was just as taken with Duncan. Soon they were taking long walks together in the evenings as well.

Their blossoming courtship obviously pleased Lady Odette, and Kendrick was not inclined to interfere as long as Duncan's duty to the mission was not hindered. He saw no signs of such. If anything, Duncan's interest in Elise seemed to settle him, tempering his restless edge and helping him focus on their work. Kendrick had come to rely on the young man's quick mind and dedication.

If only the mission were going as well as their partnership. For as weeks passed, Kendrick grew increasingly frustrated with the lack of progress in their investigation. The young people of the town declined to divulge specifics of what happened at Ra's monthly festivals and weekly fetes. The adults seemed to know very little. The need for secrecy made it difficult to ask probing questions. By the end of a month, with another festival fast approaching, he was no closer to discovering the origins of the Vincero Knights than when he first arrived.

Kendrick finally decided it was time to journey back to Chessington and report all that they knew. He informed Duncan they would stay for the upcoming festival and then depart.

"I wish you didn't have to go."

"Let's not think about that—not yet," Duncan said. "It's too beautiful a night."

The evening of the festival had turned out still and fine. Elise held Duncan's arm as they took their customary evening walk. Her closeness made him feel as though all was right in the kingdom. The cooing of the evening doves gently fell upon them while the fallen leaves swished delightfully beneath their feet. Duncan thought he could be happy in this moment forever…as long as he could forget he was leaving in two days.

"It has been good for Mother to have you and Kendrick stay with us," Elise said. "Having guests to attend to helps ease the pain of missing Father."

Duncan nodded. "Your mother is a remarkable woman." He hesitated. "Are you as pleased as she that we are here?"

Elise looked up at Duncan, her eyes gleaming in the evening light, and Duncan felt his heart skip a beat.

"No." A charming smile crossed her lips. "Even more so."

Duncan smiled more broadly than he'd intended. He couldn't help it. He had never felt like this about anyone before. He loved being with Elise, even though her presence sometimes left him feeling rather addled.

"If only you could stay," Elise said softly.

"Oh, but I will return. I am certain of it. The Council of Knights will surely want further investigation, possibly action, based on what Sir Kendrick will report."

"But if they don't?"

"Come now." Duncan scrambled to recapture the enchanted mood of the evening. "Let's not waste our last evening thinking about what may or may not happen."

Elise met his eyes and mustered a smile. She pulled gently on his arm to bring him a little closer to her as they walked. "Shall we walk as far as the Bel Lione garden?"

"It's one of my favorite places."

It took them a while to get to the manicured garden just within the town limits, but they hardly heeded the time. They strolled the garden paths as they had so many evenings before. They sat upon the ledge of a stone arched bridge that spanned a small stream and watched an early moon rise as the remnant light of the day faded away.

Duncan sighed. "It's getting dark. I should take you back."

"I suppose you're right." Elise leaned her head upon his shoulder and made no move to stand.

Duncan reached out an arm and held her close. He resisted the passing of time for a few more moments, then yielded to its endless and emotionless march across their lives.

"I do think we need to go now," she finally said. "Mother—"

"Elise!" an urgent voice shouted from the distance. "Elise!"

"Marian?" Elise called out.

They looked up to see a young woman hastily making her way toward them. Elise jumped up, a worried look on her face.

Apprehension began to swell within Duncan, for Marian came from the direction of the road that led to the castle.

Kendrick was in the stables currying Thunder when Lady Odette walked in, a troubled look on her face.

"What is it?" he asked.

"I…I'm a bit concerned. Ancel is not yet home, and it's getting late. And there is the festival—"

They exchanged a gaze that revealed thoughts neither of them wanted to speak.

"He is a good lad, my lady. I'm sure he has just been detained. I'm sure—"

"Mother! Kendrick!" Elise's voice was yet in the distance, but the urgency in her tone left no doubt that something was drastically wrong. Kendrick and Lady Odette ran to meet her in the front courtyard.

"What is it, Elise?" Lady Odette asked. "Where is Ancel?"

Elise reached for her mother's arms to steady herself. She tried to catch her breath but couldn't wait and blurted her news in broken phrases.

"Marian came to us," she gasped. "She said Ancel…went with his friends…to the festival." She paused to take a couple of deep breaths. "Duncan's gone after him, to try to stop him before he gets to the castle gate. I came for you as fast as I could. But I fear that Duncan may have gone into the castle after him."

Elise turned to Kendrick with panic in her eyes. "What will happen, Kendrick?"

Spurred by a rising dread, Kendrick turned and ran to the stables, where he grabbed Thunder's bridle. Lady Odette and Elise followed seconds later. Wordlessly they worked to help him fasten the bridle, breastplate, and crupper.

"What will happen?" Elise asked again as he led Thunder out into the courtyard.

"Stay here!" He hoisted himself into the saddle and pressed his steed into a full gallop down the road that led from the manor. A wake of leaves lifted behind Thunder's powerful strides.

Kendrick's mind raced through a thousand possibilities as he rode. All but one ended in tragedy. He fought the powerful feelings of impending doom that flooded his soul, for this ride felt like one that had occurred ten years before—right before the discovery that all but destroyed his life.

No, Duncan...no! he pleaded in his mind as his horse charged forward...forward to the castle of Bel Lione! 🔲

CHAPTER EIGHT

A PLACE
OF DESPAIR

 Duncan ran through the eastern streets of Bel Lione until he reached Lure Road. He could now see the castle, which even from this distance loomed large in the dusk. He wondered if there was any chance of stopping Ancel before he got to the castle, for it must have taken a fair amount of time for Ancel's friend Marian to reach them in the garden.

He ran until his chest hurt and his legs began to feel weak. With each stride, Lord Ra's castle loomed larger before him, an ominous fortress of towering spires that warned the wary and beckoned the foolish.

Numerous groups of young people shared the castle road with Duncan. He questioned them all about Ancel until he got an answer. Ancel had entered the castle with two other boys over an hour ago.

"Foolish boy!" Duncan muttered. Then he shook his head, realizing he sounded just like Kendrick.

Duncan took a moment to recover from his run and consider his options. Then he walked a short distance into the thick trees that bordered Lure Road to the left and found a place to hide his sword. He hesitated before loosing his hand from the hilt, feeling he was abandoning his protection and his reason at the same time, but the urgency of the moment forced him onward.

For once in his life, Duncan was grateful for his youthful features. He mussed his curly hair, put on a naive grin, and joined a group of boys heading for the castle gates. Duncan stuck to the middle of the pack as they passed two armed warriors standing guard at the near side of the drawbridge, then two more guarding the massive castle gate. Duncan held his breath but managed to pass into the castle's spacious inner yard without being apprehended. He stood with heart pounding, knowing Kendrick would be furious with his decision, no matter the outcome. But surely the immediate danger to Ancel outweighed his commitment to Kendrick to exercise caution.

Duncan scanned the castle yard, where thousands of youth milled about. Hundreds of torches lined the castle walls, illuminating bright banners. Several consorts of musicians played for clusters of dancing youth, and dozens of banquet-sized tables overflowed with meats, wine, and fruit. Cheers rose from a fenced-off arena just ahead, where groups of young people competed in some sort of sporting event. In the shadows, others paired off to flirt with each other.

The gala celebration was like no other that Duncan had ever seen. He was momentarily dazzled by the opulence of it all…and surprised by the powerful pull upon his heart to join in and indulge himself. Then he looked to the far side of the castle and was immediately shaken from the lure of the castle's torrid temptations.

A gallery surrounded the exterior of the great hall, overlooking the castle yard and games arena. A lone figure stood there, peering intently down upon the festivities. Duncan was too far away to see the man's face, but he seemed to watch the festival with a predator's pleasure. Duncan's mind was awakened to something great and evil happening that was masked by the delectable food and enticing music.

"Duncan!"

He turned to his left and saw Ancel pushing through the crowd toward him.

"Duncan, what are you—?"

Duncan grabbed the boy before he could say more and pulled him into a congested area far from the gate guards.

"Are you all right?" Duncan asked Ancel, trying not to sound too angry.

"I'm fine, but I want to get out of here." Ancel glanced toward the sports arena. Duncan thought he looked like a frightened pup.

"This place is—"

"I know," Duncan said. "Follow me."

The two walked to the gate, and Duncan held his head a little straighter as he approached. The two guards stepped in front of them, halting their exit.

"No one is allowed to leave until morning!" one of the guards said sternly.

Duncan considered making a run for it, but with the two massive warriors guarding the end of the drawbridge, he knew that their flight would be short.

"My friend's not feeling well," Duncan said. "I need to take him home."

Ancel put his hand to his stomach and winced.

"I'll take him to the infirmary." The guard grabbed Ancel's shoulder.

"No!" Duncan pulled the guard's hand away. "I'll take care of him." He put an arm around Ancel and led him away from the guards, feeling suspicious stares on them as they went.

They had gone but a few paces when they heard the thunder of a horse's hooves on the wooden planks of the drawbridge. Duncan turned to see the guards stiffen to attention as a mighty knight in armor rode through the gates. An azure cape hung from his shoulders and draped about the haunches of his steed.

"Where is Lord Ra?" the knight demanded as he reined in his horse. A guard pointed to the gallery across the yard. The knight raised his visor, peered toward the gallery, then looked down at the participants of the festival. Duncan realized the man's identity only when their eyes met in a frozen gaze.

Duncan broke eye contact and whisked Ancel through the crowd, hoping to lose themselves as quickly as possible. His heart pounded, and he could not help feeling that the walls of the castle were beginning to collapse on them. The spacious castle yard now felt like a small stone cell with nowhere to run.

"We must separate, and you must mingle with the others until morning," Duncan told Ancel urgently.

"But I want to stay with you."

"No!" Duncan grabbed Ancel's shoulder. "It isn't safe for you to be near me. Get out of here at first light. Do you understand?"

"Yes...but what's wrong?"

Duncan ignored the question and hurried away to hide among the frolicking bodies. He kept moving and stayed in the shadows as much as possible, hoping that morning would come quicker than calamity. But soon he spotted two large warriors moving youth aside to make their way to him. He instinctively reached for his sword, but his empty belt was a stark reminder of what he now knew to be a foolish decision. He had nowhere to run, no way to defend himself, and no one to help him.

The two warriors approached with scowls on their scarred faces. Each grabbed one of his upper arms, their powerful fingers nearly piercing his skin. None of the revelers seemed to notice as the warriors dragged Duncan across the castle yard into a chamber on the southeast side of the castle.

Once Duncan was inside and the door closed, the warriors slammed him up against the gray stones of the wall. One of them drew a long dagger and held it to his throat. Duncan tried to swallow against the steel of the blade, but could not do it without cutting his throat. A fear he had never known welled up within him as he looked into the warrior's vicious eyes.

"Lord Ra will want to see him *before* he is unable to speak." The voice came from a darkened corner of the room. Sir Casimir stepped forward and into the light.

The warrior holding the dagger snarled and looked at Casimir, then back at Duncan.

"Tell Lord Ra we have him," Casimir said. The other warrior left.

Casimir approached Duncan. He slowly shook his head and said with a wry smile, "You will die here, foolish knight."

The warrior pressed the dagger further against Duncan's skin and began to chuckle in anticipation. Duncan tried to turn his head away, but he could press no further into the stone wall. He began to gasp for each breath as the reality of his impending demise bore down on him. The distorted face of the warrior before him left no shred of hope beyond that of a quick death.

The door to the hall opened, and a dark figure entered. Even from across the room, Duncan could feel the evil power it emanated.

Casimir bowed low as Lord Ra strode past him toward Duncan, his black cape snapping behind him. He was outfitted in partial armor that was dark gray with red etchings. Duncan sank deeper into despair as he recognized the image engraved on Ra's breastplate—the same dragon he had seen on the Vincero medallion. Ra stepped nearer, and Duncan gazed into darkened eyes that made him tremble.

"Gorrock, that's no way to treat a guest." Lord Ra's deep voice reverberated through the chamber.

"Forgive me, my lord." The warrior pulled the dagger away from Duncan's throat and stepped aside.

Duncan slumped, his hand about his throat as he took his first deep breath in a long time. Ra reached for Duncan's shoulder and straightened him to an upright position. Then he lifted Duncan's chin slightly, inspecting him as one would a horse before making a purchase.

Duncan willed himself to look back—or up, for Lord Ra was as tall as his guards and perhaps even a bit broader. Glossy black hair hung down to just above his shoulders and only partially hid a deep scar that ran diagonally from above his left eye to his cheek. There was no question in Duncan's mind that Ra was a lofty and dark power in Lucius's evil regime.

"So this is one of His followers." Ra smirked. "He looks as puny as the rest of them." Ra looked over at Casimir. "Are you sure?"

"I am," Casimir responded.

Without looking back, Ra moved an enormous hand to Duncan's throat and slowly began to squeeze. Panic washed over Duncan, followed by an uncanny sense of calm. From somewhere came the realization that Ra and his minions feared only one thing…the power of the Prince. And he belonged to the Prince.

"I am a Knight of the—" Duncan began, but Ra's grip tightened and stopped his words.

"There is no Prince here, knave!" Ra's face was a grotesque contortion of evil. "I rule this region, and Lucius rules this kingdom. The feeble efforts of the Prince through His pitiful knights will only make us stronger, and He will one day bow before *us* in humiliation!"

Duncan strained against Ra's grip with both hands but could not break his hold. Ra leaned closer, fixing Duncan with a glare of hate and loathing. Then he released his grip and threw Duncan to the floor.

Gasping, Duncan raised himself up to one knee. "I will…tell you nothing," he managed to say.

Ra sneered. "Don't be so naive as to think you know something I don't. No, the torture you will endure is for one purpose only—our pleasure! Gorrock, take your time killing him…but *do* kill him!"

Duncan heard the guttural laugh of evil and glimpsed a movement from the corner of his eye just before a rivet-lined boot struck his face. The force knocked him onto his back, and he felt something pop in his neck.

The two warriors grabbed him and dragged him into a back chamber, then down a staircase that led into the depths of the castle. The putrid smell of death permeated his nostrils as he stumbled through musty corridors, pulled along by merciless escorts who reveled in the anticipation of his abuse.

I am so afraid, my Prince… Please help me. Duncan called out with his mind to the only One who could possibly reach into such a place of despair and hear his plea.

CHAPTER NINE

OR IN PERIL

 Kendrick rode at full gallop through the streets of Bel Lione and all the way to the castle. He slowed only as he approached the near side of the drawbridge, where two guards stepped out and crossed their poleaxes in front of him.

"I want to see Lord Ra," Kendrick demanded.

"He doesn't want to see you," one of the men replied, and they both took a more aggressive posture. "Leave at once!"

Kendrick looked closely at the misshapen faces and looming forms. These were no ordinary guards, but Shadow Warriors, servants of the Dark Knight. That in itself was proof that Lord Ra served Lucius…and confirmation that Duncan's danger was grave.

He glanced about, wondering if there was any alternate way of gaining entrance to the castle. He wasn't sure what he would do if he did gain access, but doing nothing simply wasn't an option.

He looked past the warriors to the castle behind them. Seven massive stone towers stood as guardians to their lord. Within the double walls Kendrick could see towers rising even taller than those protecting its perimeter. The gatehouse complex, or barbican, was formidable in itself, with two gate towers supporting each side of the entrance. Two portcullises made of iron grating guarded the entrance, and a large wooden drawbridge spanned the moat that encircled most of the castle.

"I am Sir Kendrick of—"

"We know who you are," spat out the guard to the right. "And you are a complete fool to approach the castle of Lord Ra. He is far too powerful to be concerned with the likes of you."

Kendrick was about to speak when he saw something flash out of the corner of his eye. He turned his head to see the deadly arc of the other guard's poleax racing toward him. Kendrick instinctively pulled hard on Thunder's reins, turning the horse toward the approaching blade. Thunder reared and turned just as the weapon finished its flight and embedded itself deep in the horse's chest and shoulder.

The sound of parting flesh and crunching bone preceded the wounded animal's distressing cries. Thunder's forelimbs collapsed, and he pitched forward upon his wounded chest and shoulder. The ax was lodged so deeply in his body that it was jerked from the hands of the warrior.

In the flash of a moment, Kendrick drew his sword as his horse continued its plummet to the ground. The animal hit with a thud, and Kendrick rolled to escape the crushing weight and thrashing hooves. He rose up on one knee just in time to see the other guard executing a vertical cut toward his head. Kendrick brought a crosscut with his sword to meet the handle of the poleax, deflecting its path enough to miss him.

The guard let the ax sink deeply into the ground and left it there as he drew a grisly sword from his scabbard. The other guard had done the same. Kendrick stood between two massive, sword-wielding foes, breathing hard and listening to his horse's final thrashes behind him. A wave of sadness shot through him, and he drew in a deep breath, deliberately setting aside his grief. There would be time later to mourn the animal who had been his faithful companion on many missions.

The right-hand guard stepped forward. "Lord Ra rules here, knave, and your blood on our swords will prove it!"

Kendrick assumed the window swordsman stance, which heralded to his enemies that he was unshaken by their taunts. No fear disturbed his thoughts, for he had something great and powerful to draw upon. "Though my blood may spill, I am not afraid of you. I have the promise of the Prince. By His name and by His power you will be defeated, for the King reigns…and His Son!"

At the mere mention of the Prince, the warriors winced, and their swords lowered slightly as though a portion of their strength left them. Then one of them yelled in defiance and advanced on Kendrick. He deflected the cut and countered quickly with his own, hoping to recover before the opposite warrior could execute an attack from behind. At the end of the maneuver he stepped quickly to the right, hoping to keep both warriors in view. How long could one man prevail against two non-Arrethtraen enemies?

He heard another yell and readied for an attack from the other warrior, then realized the cry came from the woods behind them. Another massive figure, brandishing a silver sword, emerged from the shadows of the trees and engaged one of the Shadow Warriors. Surprise and relief washed over Kendrick, for his new and unidentified ally brought new hope to the fight.

Kendrick focused on his foe as the sounds of intense and steady crashes of steel upon steel filled the night air. His opponent's cuts were powerful, but Kendrick held his own and relied on his speed and agility to balance the fight. Not knowing who had joined him or what the other man's skill level was, Kendrick assumed the worst and considered his ally's appearance as merely a helpful distraction.

Kendrick deflected a horizontal cut and parried a thrust. He then countered with an intense combination that put his opponent in retreat. He landed a slice on the warrior's left arm, which brought a yell and a curse from the lips of the Shadow Warrior. Kendrick could tell that the wound was deep and was amazed at how little it seemed to affect the warrior.

"Silent Warriors!" Kendrick heard the other warrior yell to the castle gate, but they were his last words. The blade of Kendrick's mysterious friend found its mark, and the Shadow Warrior collapsed to the ground. Kendrick's opponent began retreating toward the castle just as footsteps pounded on the drawbridge behind him.

"We cannot let him tell the castle I was here," Kendrick's large ally said and moved to engage the first Shadow Warrior.

Kendrick joined the fight and moved to one side to divert attention, but the Shadow Warrior seemed more concerned with the sword of Kendrick's large friend. This allowed Kendrick the opportunity to execute a thrust that put the warrior down.

"Follow me," the large fellow said.

Kendrick wasted no time as they plunged into the depths of the nearby forest, just ahead of Lord Ra's guards. Kendrick had to work hard to stay up with the form ahead of him, who seemed to glide easily through the trees and brush despite his size. Kendrick's mind filled with questions as he blindly followed this unusual ally. The loss of his steed also pressed back upon him, and he worried he would never find an equal.

They ran for some time before the big man stopped and motioned Kendrick to silence. They waited and listened, then continued their flight on a wooded uphill path. Finally they stopped in a small clearing. Kendrick turned to fully face his mysterious ally for the first time.

The man was as large as the guards at the castle bridge. His skin was black, and there was not a hair upon his head. His huge physique was a picture of sculpted athletic perfection, and his eyes glowed like burning coals. But though his size was daunting and his countenance fierce, Kendrick sensed he was someone to trust and not fear.

"Thank you for coming to my aid, sir." He bowed. "May I ask your name?"

The warrior glared at him. "I heard you proclaim the King and His Son, and as a Silent Warrior I was honor-bound to come to your aid.

You were foolish to approach Lord Ra's castle alone!" His deep voice carried an unusual accent.

Kendrick had heard of the Prince's secret force of Silent Warriors, but he had never encountered one until now. His gaze fell to the forest floor at hearing the Silent Warrior's rebuke.

"I'm sure you are right," he answered quietly. "But a fellow knight is in peril. Would you have reacted so differently if a fellow warrior's life was in jeopardy?" Kendrick looked back up at the warrior.

The warrior did not reply, but his countenance softened slightly. "I am Bronwyn. Why are you here?"

"Initially to verify the origin of a Vincero Knight we've identified, but now…" Kendrick paused. "Now I'm here because my fellow knight went into the festival tonight to save a friend from the influences of Lord Ra."

Bronwyn shook his head and seemed all the more perturbed. "You saw the Vincero Knight's medallion?"

"Not I, but Duncan, my comrade. Who are these knights?"

"They are Arrethtraen men and women who belong to a secret order of knights created by Lucius and trained to exercise his power and control over the people. They can be as ruthless as the Shadow Warriors. The one you identified—are you sure that he is from this region?"

"We believe he is. The map on his medallion bore a mark in the area around Bel Lione," Kendrick said. "And the letters *R* and *A* were engraved on the back."

"Then there is little hope for your friend," the warrior said. "He is probably already dead."

The words confirmed the fears of Kendrick's heart, yet they hit him like a battle-ax. "Why?"

Bronwyn looked sternly at Kendrick. "Because it is nearly impossible to deceive Ra. He is shrewd, intelligent, informed, and very powerful. If this Vincero Knight you speak of is in the castle, then…" Bronwyn turned to leave without finishing his sentence.

"Surely there is *something* that can be done!" Kendrick cried in desperation. His mind turned back to the discovery of his murdered wife and child. At that time, everything in his being had wanted to right the wrong and he had ached to launch into action, but there had been no way to alter the tragedy. This situation was almost worse, for he didn't know if the tragedy had yet come to pass, and his soul screamed to stop it.

Bronwyn shook his head. "Ra is too strong."

Fury rose in Kendrick's bosom, and he refused to accept the apparent victory of the Prince's dark foe. He grabbed Bronwyn's massive arm and pulled the Silent Warrior back to face him once again.

"I don't know if my friend is dead or yet alive," he exclaimed. "But I do know this bastion of evil Lord Ra has built cannot stand, and I will dedicate every breath of my life to destroying it. I will not rest until every last stone is torn from its walls and every one of Ra's evil warriors is destroyed. You say that Ra is too strong, but I don't believe it. I say the *Prince* is too strong—too strong to let this monster continue to tear the youth of this land from the arms of their mothers and the hearts of their fathers. Too strong to let these Vincero Knights spread like disease from Lucius's—"

Bronwyn suddenly reached down and grabbed Kendrick's tunic in the center of his chest. With one powerful push, the Silent Warrior slammed him up against a tree.

Kendrick nearly lost his breath and wondered at Bronwyn's response.

Bronwyn held his grip tightly and leaned down so his face was just inches from Kendrick's. His eyes narrowed, as though he were peering into the portals of Kendrick's soul, transmitting something deep and personal.

Kendrick felt powerless in his grip, though his heart didn't retreat.

"I have watched as Ra built this castle stone by stone." Bronwyn's voice was hushed, yet furious. "I have watched as young men and women succumbed to his deceptions and sold their souls to his ways. I have watched as the Vincero Knights were deployed to work Ra's evil will. For many years I have watched…and waited. I have seen the weakness of Arrethtraens and waited for strength to come. You are the first Knight of the Prince I have made contact with."

Bronwyn slowly relaxed his grip on Kendrick. "When the Prince came to Arrethtrae and died and rose again, I did not understand His ways. Only now do I begin to see, for I see His power burning within you, as it must be in so many others."

Bronwyn released Kendrick completely and stepped back. He walked to the edge of the clearing and stared at Lord Ra's castle, visible in the moonlight through the trees.

"My waiting seemed futile," he murmured, "until now."

Kendrick moved away from the tree, still slightly shaken. "How long have you known Ra?"

Bronwyn still stared toward the castle, but Kendrick could tell that he was seeing something else…something older.

"Since the beginning. His name was once Ramsey…before the rebellion…when he was my friend." Bronwyn fell into silence, and Kendrick waited. Finally Bronwyn turned and looked at him.

"Ramsey was closer than a brother to me. Then slowly something began to change, and I didn't realize what was happening to him until it was too late. The thought that Lucius, our own commander, would persuade the loyal warriors of the King to join him in a rebellion was inconceivable. I see it now, but then…it just didn't seem possible. In a single night the friendship of a brother became the enmity of a foe." Bronwyn slowly shook his head, as if he was trying to clear a bad dream.

"Have you ever tried to talk to him?" Kendrick asked. "To persuade him to come back?"

"Once, and I nearly died for it. The Ramsey who was my friend is forever gone. The minds and souls of the Silent Warriors who joined Lucius in that rebellion against the King and the Prince so long ago have become warped and twisted. Some may now understand the foolishness of their choice, but they fear Lucius's power over them and obey him without question. Others have taken up the banner of rebellion whole-heartedly and become powerful enemies of the Prince."

Bronwyn sighed. "Such is the case with Rams—Ra. With each passing day, I watched him become more evil and dark. My mission of observation has been difficult, for the heinous acts he has committed against the King and His people have stirred great anger within my heart. Ra must be stopped!" Bronwyn's huge hands tightened into fists, and Kendrick felt the urge to step back and away from this powerful vessel of the King.

Kendrick eyed the castle. Its towering spires seemed so much more ominous. He marveled at how different it looked from when they first arrived. No longer did it beautify the city and the surrounding hills. He thought of Duncan within its dark and lofty walls. "Surely there is *something* that can be done."

Bronwyn stared at him in silence for a moment. "Go to Morley the cooper. If there is any chance of saving your friend, he may have useful information." Bronwyn once again turned to leave.

"That's all?" Kendrick asked, wondering how far he could push the warrior.

Bronwyn looked over his shoulder at Kendrick. "I have lost friends in this battle, Sir Kendrick. You will too." Bronwyn disappeared into the shadowy curtains of the forest.

CHAPTER TEN

THE PECULIAR
MR. MORLEY

 Kendrick did not wait for morning, for each passing moment could be Duncan's last. As soon as he found his way back to town, he knocked on the cooper's door, hoping the man would hear him from his quarters above his barrel-making shop. After numerous attempts, each one more intense than the last, Kendrick yielded to the probability that no one was home. He went to nearby shops, trying to find someone who might know if Morley was near.

"There's no tellin' where that crazy buffoon might be. If the lamp isn't lit, you'll not find 'im till tomorrow," the shop owner across the street said crossly and then slammed the door.

Kendrick returned to the cooper's shop and knocked once more. This time he was rewarded with the sound of an irregular pattern of footsteps. As they grew louder, the light emanating from the crack beneath the doorway brightened slightly. The creak of the bolt being loosened from its lock seemed loud in the quiet of the night, and the door opened just enough for an eye to stare out.

"What ya wantin'?" came a voice laced with irritation.

"I am Kendrick of Penwell. May I talk with you for a moment?"

The man muttered something beneath his breath, but the door opened. Kendrick stepped inside, and the man held a lamp up high to get a look at him. Kendrick could also now see Mr. Morley more clearly. He was an odd-looking fellow, well beyond middle age, with a hunched back, a long nose, and ears a little large for his thin face and frail-looking body. As he inspected Kendrick, he pursed his lips tightly together, and they protruded out nearly to the tip of his nose. Kendrick had obviously roused him from sleep, and his disgust at the intrusion was clear. As he became more alert, Morley's eyes opened wider, and Kendrick got the sense that the man was as peculiar within as he was without.

"Mr. Morley, I have come to you because—"

"I can see in your face that you have lost one to Lord Ra…like so many before you. Others have come to me, but I can offer them nothing except this: the choice was their own, and their own shall they bear." Morley set the lamp on a nearby table and walked toward a counter near one of the walls. "Mourn not for the foolish, though they be your sons or daughters, for darkness swallows all who play in its shadows."

Kendrick tried to ignore the feeling that this visit to Mr. Morley would be a futile exercise. "You don't understand, sir. I have not lost a son or daughter, but a fellow Knight…of the Prince."

Morley stopped with his back to Kendrick. He slowly turned around, shuffled back to the table, and leaned across the lamp to look deep into Kendrick's eyes. The light of the lamp illuminated Morley's face from below, giving Kendrick the bizarre impression that he was looking and talking to a floating head.

Morley squinted, and he pointed a gnarled finger at Kendrick's chest. "If that is true, then *I* am the foolish one, for I could be killed just for speaking to you."

Morley continued to stare at Kendrick, then smacked his lips together as though he were chewing something. "When did your friend go into the castle?"

"Just tonight, to save a boy. But I think—"

"There is nothing to be done tonight. Your only hope is that he returns to you tomorrow. I cannot help you."

Morley picked up the lamp and headed toward the door. Kendrick followed, protesting. "But he may be dead by tomorrow!"

Morley opened the door and held the light up closely to his face. His eyes looked wild, almost as if he delighted in the thought of Duncan's demise.

"Yes," Morley said slowly and waited for Kendrick to leave.

Kendrick bit back an angry retort, realizing it would make little difference to this strange fellow. *Why would Bronwyn waste my time by sending me here?*

He walked the remaining distance to Lionsgate, where the lanterns still burned and the two women waited anxiously. He told them of the evening's events. Then they settled in for a sleepless night.

At sunrise Lady Odette served them breakfast, but most of the food remained untouched. Elise finally excused herself from the table and escaped to the front porch, where she slowly paced from one end to the other. Kendrick remained and tried to comfort Lady Odette.

Long after their food had grown cold, Kendrick heard Elise call from the porch. "Ancel comes!"

The three of them ran into the front courtyard and down the roadway toward Ancel. Lady Odette greeted her son as though he had come back from the dead.

He pulled back from her embrace, his eyes full of sorrow. "I'm so sorry, Mother."

Elise grabbed Ancel's arm. "Where is Duncan?"

Ancel looked at Elise. There was great pain in his countenance.

"Where?" Elise shouted and shook his arm.

Ancel's chin dropped to his chest. "He is in the castle."

Elise's hand fell to her side, as though it carried the weight of a heavy stone. She began to weep softly. Kendrick turned away, for he didn't want to show the severity of his anger or his concern.

"I'm sorry, El." Ancel's voice quivered. "I didn't think anyone would come into the castle looking for me. I…" His voice trailed off to silence.

Elise turned and ran into the manor. Kendrick turned about and looked at Ancel. "Did you see Duncan?"

"Yes."

"Tell me everything you saw, Ancel—everything!"

The boy covered his face with his hands.

"You must tell Sir Kendrick everything," Lady Odette said, "if there is to be any hope of helping Duncan."

Ancel dropped his hands from his face, and his eyes were red. He blinked a few times and gathered himself to share his story.

"My friends and I entered the castle around the ninth hour. I didn't want to become like them—truly, Mother. I just wanted to see what the festival was like and learn more about Lord Ra. He was just inside the gate, smiling and greeting all who entered. The castle was full of music and dancing and all kinds of food and drink. At first it seemed like a wonderful celebration. There were hundreds and hundreds of us, maybe thousands…I don't know. I ate some, but mostly I just watched. After a couple of hours, the celebration became quite…ah…unruly." Ancel lowered his eyes again. "Many became drunk from the strong ale. Things began to happen that made me very uncomfortable."

"What kinds of things?" Kendrick asked.

"They began to burn strange incense, and people became affectionate with each other. Even the sporting games turned dreadful."

"How so?" Kendrick asked.

Ancel frowned as he recalled the images for Kendrick. "At first there were contests of skill that tested strength and accuracy with the sword. But then Lord Ra ordered that wild pigs be brought in for the participants to practice on. Everyone cheered as the blood flowed, but Lord Ra seemed to enjoy it the most. He watched most of the festival from up above, on the gallery. He's frightful, Mother, just as Father suspected."

Ancel looked to Lady Odette for some assurance that he had not completely lost her trust or her love. She reached down and took his hand in hers, nodding for him to continue.

"I began to feel sick from the sights and smells and wanted to leave, so I started toward the castle gate." Ancel looked at Kendrick now. "That's when I saw Duncan enter. I was so glad to see him. I ran over to him and told him I wanted to get out of the castle, but the warriors inside the gate wouldn't let us out. They said no one could leave until sunrise.

"Just then a mounted knight entered through the gate, and Duncan became very nervous—almost afraid. He said I shouldn't be seen with him there and pushed me into a crowd of people. He said I should stay away from the castle guards until morning and then get out. Then I lost track of him. He just disappeared!"

"That was the last you saw of him?"

Ancel shook his head. "A little while later, I saw the same knight talking with Lord Ra up on the gallery. The knight pointed, and soon two huge guards took Duncan deeper into the castle. And...I didn't know what to do."

The boy stared at Kendrick with tears in his eyes. "I should have gone after him. I know that. But I...was afraid. So I did what Duncan told me to. I waited until sunrise and got out as fast as I—"

Kendrick interrupted. "What were the colors of the knight you saw?"

Ancel thought for a moment. "They were gold and blue."

Kendrick closed his eyes and nodded, certain the man could be none other than Sir Casimir. He struggled to put aside his anger at both Ancel *and* Duncan, knowing such a response would do no one any good. He needed to act quickly instead of indulging his feelings.

The trouble was, he had no idea what action to take next.

He considered riding to Chessington for help, but it would be at least two weeks, and Duncan would surely be dead by then, if he wasn't already. Besides, it would take more than just a few knights to gain access to the castle. It would take an army.

He considered his options a moment longer, then turned to leave.

"What are you going to do?" Ancel asked.

"I'm going to talk to a crazy old man again. Lady Odette, I will need a horse."

She didn't hesitate. "Take Pilgrim."

Kendrick knew that Pilgrim was her late husband's horse, a well-muscled chestnut. Although he had been put to farm work in recent years, he had trained to carry a knight into battle. Kendrick opened his mouth with the intention of refusing her offer, but she held up her hand.

"He yearns to be the steed of a knight once again. Take him and go!"

"Thank you, my lady. I shall take good care of him."

Lady Odette nodded, and Kendrick ran to prepare the horse.

Once under saddle, Pilgrim seemed to sense the urgency and importance of their mission. He carried his new rider smoothly and swiftly into town and to the cooper's shop, where Kendrick heard a ferocious exchange of contemptuous words between the cooper and a customer.

"Your barrels leaked," the customer said smugly.

"Liar!" Morley exclaimed. "Liar, liar, liar!" He pounded his fist on a barrel to emphasize each word. Spittle sprayed from his lips as he spoke. His eyes were wild and full of anger. "You'll pay the full price o' those barrels or I'll—"

"Or you'll what?" The man puffed up his chest and looked scornfully down on Morley's hunched form.

Morley muttered something incomprehensible.

"That's what I thought." The man placed four coins on the barrel between them. "Take half or nothing at all."

Morley leaned over the barrel and eyed the coins. He grabbed them and then pointed a crooked finger at the customer. "You are a thief an' a liar."

The man retreated one step to avoid more flying spittle.

"I'll never make another barrel for you. Be gone from here!"

The man rolled his eyes and left.

Kendrick hesitated just a moment to let the mood settle, then stepped forward.

"You again," Morley said gruffly. "What do you want?"

"My friend did not return."

"I've already told ya that I got nothin' to help you." Morley placed the coins into his money box and turned about. Pursing his lips in the same odd fashion, he lifted his chin a bit to look more directly at Kendrick. The cooper's eyes looked as wild as they had the night before.

"Are you for Lord Ra or against him?" Kendrick asked.

The old man laughed. "I am neither for nor against, just a witness t' the passing o' night upon the land."

Kendrick placed two gold coins on the table. "If that be so, then be a witness for me and tell me how I can save my friend."

Morley cackled as if to make jest of Kendrick, but he picked up the gold coins and eyed them carefully before placing them in his pocket. "I can't tell you how to save your friend. But I can tell you which mountain to climb." Morley pointed a gnarled finger at Kendrick's face and laughed again.

Kendrick narrowed his eyes and waited for more. The man was surely mad, but Kendrick was desperate enough to listen even to the ravings of a madman.

"There is a man who does not exist," Morley said with a gleam in his eye. "But I can tell you where to find him!"

Kendrick listened and found himself a prisoner to the one shred of hope given him by the wild-eyed cooper of Bel Lione. By midday, Kendrick had set his course for the Northern Mountains. ◈

CHAPTER ELEVEN

LOYALTY'S COURAGE

 The Northern Mountains lay a two days' ride to the northwest—a far more rugged range than the gentler peaks surrounding Bel Lione. Morley the cooper had insisted that Kendrick make his search on foot, so he found a small farm at the base of the range to quarter Pilgrim. Then he began the arduous climb, following the directions the wild-eyed Mr. Morley had given him.

By the day's end, Kendrick was partway up one of the peaks, high enough to feel the bite of snow on his feet. His breath swirled up as white vapor in the evening mountain air as he stopped to look around him. He was sure that he was at the place Morley had told him of, for the landmarks matched the description perfectly, but there was no evidence of the dwelling Morley had described.

He traversed an area of snow-covered rocks and then passed through a stand of pine trees that released their burden of snow when he jostled the branches. When the pines thinned, he spotted a high ledge and decided to climb toward it to gain a better vantage point. As he stood there plotting his course, he heard a familiar sound, the creak of leather binding upon itself.

Someone close behind was recoiling for a strike with a weapon.

The next instant, Kendrick heard the tightened leather clothing of his attacker release and realized he could not escape the blade. Assuming his attacker was right-handed, Kendrick quickly withdrew his sword from his scabbard and inverted it, holding it vertically along his right shoulder with the hilt raised slightly above his head. He braced his shoulder against the flat of his own blade just as the sword of his unseen foe slammed against it.

Angry with himself for being taken by surprise, Kendrick whirled to face his opponent. But before he could fully position himself, he had to thwart another slice and then a thrust. Kendrick countered the blows and then attacked, hoping to bring a pause to the brief but intense fight and get a better look at his unknown enemy.

The man before him was at least twenty years his senior. His closely trimmed beard was white, his flowing hair nearly so, but his body was well muscled, and he possessed the fierce demeanor of an experienced fighter. His purpose seemed singular—to kill Kendrick quickly.

"I come in peace!" Kendrick exclaimed as the blades flew.

The man didn't seem to listen. He just used the pause to recover and then launch another furious volley of cuts and slices. Kendrick matched his opponent's attack, realizing the engagement might well end with someone's blood staining the white snow beneath their feet. He settled into the fight and searched for the rhythm of this man's battle.

It was a masterful duel. Soon both men were breathing hard, and the thick white vapor of their breath testified to their exertion. After a lengthy time of fighting, Kendrick was able to take advantage of a split-second break in the man's defense. He thrust through the opening but pulled up short before his sword could pierce the man's side. Then he retreated and paused once again.

The man hesitated, for it was obvious to a swordsman of such expertise that Kendrick had purposely held back from drawing blood.

"I do not come to harm you," Kendrick said, "but to ask for your help."

This time the man replied not with his sword, but with a skeptical look. "Vincero Knights do not ask for help. They come only to kill." Without warning, he launched another attack.

Kendrick defended and countered. "I am not a Vincero Knight," he shouted above the clash of swords. "I am a Knight of the Prince."

The fight paused again. "I know of no such order," the man said.

Kendrick thought of Duncan and felt the urgency of his mission again. He looked the man in the eye. Then, very slowly, he lowered his sword and opened his arms. He took a great risk in doing so, for he would find it difficult to recover in time if the man chose to take advantage of his evident vulnerability.

"We are an order of peace...and of hope," Kendrick explained to his opponent. "We have only one enemy—Lucius the Dark Knight and his Shadow Warriors."

This statement visibly stunned the man, and his sword lowered slightly. "What is your name?"

"I am Kendrick of Penwell."

The man hesitated, not completely relinquishing his defensive posture.

Kendrick opened his arms wider. "I am at your mercy, sir, for I come on behalf of a fellow knight. His life and now mine will be determined by your choice this moment."

The man hesitated. "Remove your breastplate." He tightened his grip on his sword as if to ready himself for an attack.

Kendrick sensed he needed to trust this man, yet struggled with the courage to do so. He thrust the tip of his sword into the snow in front of him with the hilt still within arm's reach. Then he removed his breastplate and let it fall to the ground.

The man approached slowly, never taking his gaze from Kendrick's eyes. He reached up with his left hand, grabbed Kendrick's tunic by the collar, and pulled it down to expose Kendrick's chest to the chill of the mountain air. His gaze slowly dropped to Kendrick's chest—as if probing his heart for his true intentions—then back up to his eyes. Finally he released his grasp on Kendrick's tunic and stepped back.

"I am Landor," he said. "Come with me."

Relief flooded through Kendrick as he recovered his breastplate, sheathed his sword, and moved to follow the other man through the snow. Landor walked quickly, despite a slight limp in his gait. He led them deeper into the mountain forest, climbing steadily until eventually they reached a steep and rocky cliff. Once they had scaled it, Kendrick turned about and realized he could see the entire southern approach of the mountain range from this vantage point. Another fifty paces on, behind a thick curtain of pine trees, stood a small secluded cabin.

Kendrick entered behind Landor and discovered a comfortable, neatly kept dwelling. There was only one room, for the place was obviously meant to shelter but a single man. It appeared to Kendrick that Landor had lived here for a very long time.

"Sit." Landor pointed to the single chair next to his table. He placed some bread and an urn of water on the table between them, then retrieved a stool from the corner and sat across from Kendrick.

Kendrick nodded his thanks but didn't eat or drink. Neither did Landor. He just sat and looked at Kendrick through narrowed eyes. "Regardless of the words you are about to speak, one of us will die today."

Kendrick understood instantly. Landor would kill or die rather than let anyone know of his existence or his location.

"If this is true," Kendrick replied, "then I have journeyed in vain to find you. For my quest involves saving lives, not destroying them." Kendrick met Landor's hard stare as he searched the man's deep blue eyes for the slightest hint of compassion. He found something else instead.

"How did you know to search for me here?" Landor asked. "Why did you come?"

"You can be at peace. No other sane Arrethtraen knows you live on this mountain."

Landor's brow furrowed as if he didn't understand.

"As for my purpose, I have a friend who is in great peril, and I am told that you are the only one who might be able to help me."

Landor huffed out a mirthless laugh. "I help no one." He looked away. "It is not my...purpose in life."

"I hear your words," Kendrick replied, "but I see something very different."

At that Landor looked back and nearly sneered at him.

"I am here, alive, and sitting in your cabin," Kendrick said. "Your allowance of my presence here testifies to something more in you." He leaned forward to make his argument. "You are a master swordsman, disciplined by nobility. And surely you realize that there is nothing more noble than to save the life of another."

Landor gazed down at the table. For one brief instant, the mighty man looked sad and afraid.

"Tell me, Landor, what do you fear so greatly down there"—Kendrick nodded toward the base of the mountain—"that you would die up here rather than face it?"

Landor snapped from his moment of reflection. He pushed to his feet with both hands on the table and leaned across it, his face red with defiant anger.

Kendrick wondered if their fight might resume at that instant. He kept his gaze steady. "I have felt the mastery of your sword. Even the Vincero Knights are no match for you. Why do you fear them?"

Landor's face twisted into something between anger and pain. Clenching his fists as if fighting for control, he stalked away from the table, then turned back to face Kendrick.

"I do not fear the Vinceros," he retorted with a bitter smile. He opened the top portion of his leather doublet to reveal his chest. "I am one!"

Kendrick almost stopped breathing.

On Landor's chest, over his heart, was the scarred brand of the same insignia Kendrick had seen on the medallion in Chessington.

CHAPTER TWELVE

A LIFE FOR A LIFE

Kendrick's heart pounded as he stared at Landor. He had assumed this man was hiding from the Vincero Knights. That Landor might actually be one of Lucius's evil henchmen had not occurred to him. Kendrick's eyes opened wide as he frantically considered his options. Why had he ever disarmed himself in Landor's presence?

Landor walked back to the table, and in his eyes Kendrick saw the same darkness that had shadowed Sir Casimir's face. The emblem on his chest seemed to grow larger with his approach.

Kendrick stood quickly, his chair toppling behind him as his hand flew to his sword. He instinctively backed away two steps to allow for fighting room, but this time it was Landor who did not reach for his sword.

The men faced each other across the table again. Kendrick was quite at odds as to what to do until his thoughts turned once again to Duncan. Regardless of Landor's identity, he might still be Kendrick's best and only hope for his young friend. Besides, Kendrick realized, Landor had tried to kill him because he thought he was a Vincero Knight. Remembering that helped settle Kendrick's anxiety.

Kendrick released his grip on his sword and let it stay at rest within the scabbard. He lifted his hand and took a deep breath.

"Although I do not yet know your story, Landor, it seems to me that we have mutual enemies." Kendrick slowly approached the table, lifted the urn of water, and filled both chalices. He lifted one with each hand and offered one to Landor. "Mutual enemies can create the most unusual of allies…or even friends." Kendrick softened his countenance and waited for Landor's reply.

The man hesitated and then took the chalice from Kendrick. They both drank and sat at the table again. The tension eased, and Kendrick knew the threat of battle was gone—at least for a time.

"Many years ago," Kendrick said quietly, "I lost a wife and a son to the deeds of evil men." Remembering it, he felt himself sliding back once more into grief, his voice nearly breaking as he pleaded with Landor, "Please do not force me to lose a brother to the same!"

Kendrick's gaze fell to the uneaten bread on the table and then back to Landor, whose countenance had changed. His visage of critical discernment had transformed to one of wonder. Kendrick thought perhaps his plea had uncovered a corner of the man's heart where compassion had not yet been fully purged by Lucius.

At least *something* seemed to have moved his heart. The man avoided Kendrick's eyes, staring out through the walls of his cabin and beyond to the isolation of the mountains. When he spoke, it was in a voice so low Kendrick had to lean forward to hear it.

"I have been trying to escape from the order of the Vincero Knights for a long time. But there is no place in all the kingdom where I can go. This is my seventh refuge, and I have fought many knights for my survival." Landor shook his head. "There is no hiding from Lord Ra."

Kendrick reached across the table and grabbed Landor's arm. "Your trainer was Lord Ra?"

"Yes."

Kendrick's eyes opened wide. "Bel Lione is the castle where my friend is imprisoned!"

Landor's eyes seemed fearful and sad. "If your friend is truly a prisoner there, then he is probably already dead. If not, then he wishes for death, especially if Lord Ra suspects him to be more than just a foolish commoner."

"I will do whatever it takes to save him, Landor. I have sworn it."

"You swear in vain, Kendrick. Lord Ra is more powerful and cunning than anyone in the entire kingdom. You do not know him as I do."

Kendrick gazed at Landor, thinking it strange for such a skilled man to be so defeated in his heart. He could not help the smile that formed on his lips, which obviously bewildered Landor. "There is One more powerful than Lord Ra, my friend," Kendrick said. "Much more powerful."

"That is quite impossible." Landor leaned away from the table. "Lord Ra rules all—at least in this region of the kingdom. And even if there *was* someone more powerful, I would not want to meet him, for such power would make his evil all the more unbearable."

"No, Landor. This One is just and fair and full of compassion and mercy." Kendrick could not contain his enthusiasm at being able to share the truth with a man so full of fear and despair. "He is the Prince, the Son of the King. And I am His servant!"

Landor seemed skeptical. "I have heard of a King who once ruled Arrethtrae, but I have never heard of this…this Prince." He raised one eyebrow. "Even if He exists, I can't imagine His power to be greater than that of Lord Ra."

"Landor, even Lord Ra has a lord greater than he, and the Prince could fell them both in an instant!"

"Now you speak once again of the mythical Dark Knight," Landor said.

"He is as real as Lord Ra. And so is the Prince."

Landor seemed perplexed and yet drawn to Kendrick's tale. Kendrick reached for the bread on the table. He tore off a piece and offered it to Landor. "Let me tell you of the bread that brings hope and life to all who eat of it."

Kendrick had an unusually strong feeling that the opportunity to tell this man about the Prince was inextricably tied to his ultimate purpose as a Knight of the Prince. So he told the story of the great King, Lucius's rebellion, and the King's audacious plan to save His people from the devastation wrought by Lucius.

"The King did not choose to send a great army to destroy Lucius and his Shadow Warriors, for the people of the kingdom would also have suffered greatly under such fierce battle. Instead, He chose to send His only Son, the Prince. The Prince came disguised as a pauper, looking for the good and faithful hearts of men and women who would be loyal to the King. He began to train a force of gallant men and women known as the Knights of the Prince, but His actions soon brought the attention of greedy and powerful men. They claimed He came to destroy the Code by which they lived, though in truth He was the only man ever to fulfill the Code perfectly. For this and His claim to be the King's Son, they killed Him."

"You're saying your powerful Prince is dead?"

"He was killed. But He is not dead."

"You talk in riddles, Kendrick!"

Kendrick gave Landor a look of compassion. "You were trained by Lord Ra, were you not?"

"Yes. But what does that have to do with your wild story of a Prince?"

"Would you agree that he is more powerful than any man you have ever seen?"

"Yes."

"More evil than any man you have ever seen?"

At that, Landor paused, then answered slowly. "Yes."

"Look into my eyes, Landor, and tell me that there isn't something about Lord Ra that is beyond the power and evil of a mere man of Arrethtrae." Kendrick held Landor's gaze for a moment and did not receive a response. "You know in your heart that there is something about Lord Ra that transcends us mortal Arrethtraens. Something deeper and darker…more dangerous. You've looked into his eyes and seen it…felt it! That power comes from Ra's master, for Ra has been a follower of the Dark Knight from the beginning."

Kendrick saw Landor reflect back to those times and watched him cower at his own thoughts.

"Think of it this way. For every valley, there is a mountain. For every desert, there is an ocean. For every night, there is a day. Well, for ultimate evil, there is ultimate good. And that good is the Prince!" Kendrick sat up straight and spoke boldly. "The Prince did not stay dead, you see. The King brought Him back to life, and He is waiting for the day when He will return with His mighty army of knights and warriors to reclaim Arrethtrae for the King. On that day He will rule with great power, great wisdom, and great love!"

Landor seemed quite overwhelmed, wanting to deny what seemed like a fairy tale and yet finding it impossible to deny the truth Kendrick had revealed about Lord Ra.

There was a long period of silence as Kendrick let him digest the transforming story of the Prince. Finally, Landor looked up at Kendrick, and he seemed sadder than before.

Kendrick saw his pain and thought he knew its cause. "When my wife and infant son were murdered," he said solemnly, "my whole purpose in life became to avenge their deaths. I left my home in Bremsfeld, and for many years I searched for the marauders. My quest consumed me and began to eat at my soul as a worm eats through rotten meat."

Landor's expression was unreadable. "Did you find them?"

"Some…but not all. I fought each duel with vengeance, looking to be satisfied, but it did not happen. Instead, I became a shell of a man—empty, finally just wanting to die. While wandering the streets of Penwell, I heard a man tell a strange story about a Prince. Just like you, I thought the man was mad for telling such a fairy tale as though he believed it. But in my heart I knew there was truth in his words. I discovered that the Prince forgives us for the evil we have done and gives us a new life to live…one that I am living now."

"As a Vincero Knight, my evil deeds are many and great," Landor murmured, then gazed back at Kendrick defiantly. "You say you are different for hearing the words of this Prince. What would you do if you were to find one of these marauders now?"

Kendrick hesitated, for the question was one he had not dared ask himself. This realization pierced him, for it revealed his heart, and he suspected the ground there was not as solid as he wanted it to be.

"I don't know, Landor. But I am not looking."

Landor seemed satisfied enough with the answer. He took another bite from the nearly forgotten portion of bread in his hand and followed it with a swig of water.

Nothing more was said for some time, for Kendrick knew that for a man like Landor an abundance of words would only diminish the power of those previously spoken. Landor stood and crossed over to the one small window in his cabin, one that faced south.

"Bel Lione has only one weakness," Landor said without turning around. "But Prince or no Prince, you would be a fool to try and take advantage of it."

Kendrick smiled. "Then call me a fool!"

Landor turned, and he was actually smiling. "Where Lord Ra's castle now stands, there was once a much smaller castle…with a single small chamber beneath it. On the mountain side of the castle, a secret passageway led to this lower chamber. I have been told it was an escape passage if the castle were ever to come under siege. Lord Ra destroyed the first castle and built his own in its place, expanding the small chamber underneath into a massive set of dungeons. Yet remarkably, the secret passageway was never discovered."

Landor paused and seemed to stare backward in time. "He who told me of this is dead, and no one else knows of it—not even Lord Ra."

"You're saying there is a back entrance into the castle." Kendrick struggled to keep down his excitement. "Can you show me?"

"I'll not set foot within two days' ride of that place," Landor replied. "Lord Ra has been searching for me ever since I abandoned my mission. Each time I run, I must go farther and farther away."

"Then draw a map for me," Kendrick said.

Landor shook his head as he sat and finished the last of his bread. "You really are a madman, aren't you? Your chances of even getting close to the castle are almost nil. Even if you manage to do that, you will still face Lord Ra's blood wolves. If by some miracle you do gain entrance to the dungeons, there are hundreds of passageways and chambers to search, all guarded by warriors as vicious as Ra himself. And all to rescue a friend who is probably dead already."

Kendrick just stared at Landor and would not be moved. Landor finally nodded. He found a piece of parchment and began to draw a map for Kendrick, then paused.

"It is the blood wolves that will end your rescue attempt before you begin," he said soberly.

"What are blood wolves?" Kendrick asked. "Are there many?"

"No, but there only needs to be one. Lord Ra has bred them large and vicious. They are twice as heavy as a man and ten times as deadly. Once they kill, they roll in the blood of their prey, thus the name. They are frightful creatures. If you can kill or wound one, then…" Landor shook his head again. "This is absurd. No one can survive any of this, let alone rescue someone else."

"Look at it this way, Landor. You won't have to kill me to keep your mountaintop refuge a secret."

Landor didn't laugh, and neither did Kendrick.

"Tell me more about the blood wolves," Kendrick said. "How do you know so much about them?"

"Before I was a Vincero Knight, it was my duty to help breed them." Landor stood and placed his right leg on the chair. He lifted his trouser leg to reveal a long, jagged scar that started behind his knee and ran to his ankle.

"That is when they are at their worst, if there is such a thing as worse than a nightmare." Landor ran his right hand down the scar, as if trying to soothe some residual ache, then he sat down. "Have you taken a torch into the woods and seen the glowing eyes of animals at night?"

"Yes."

"That doesn't happen with these beasts. They have no pupils."

Kendrick was surprised. "How do they see?"

"They don't. They smell, listen, and feel."

"Feel?" Kendrick tilted his head.

"Since they are blind, which was one of the results of Lord Ra's breeding, they have compensated by feeling the ground, almost like a spider feels its web. They lie in half burrows with their abdomens and four paws touching the earth, feeling for slight vibrations. I've seen them sense the steps of a man a hundred paces away. As they move closer to their prey, they use their sense of smell and hearing to finish the hunt. Once an animal—or a man—enters the domain of one of these creatures, it doesn't come out."

"Surely a swift sword or a lance could defeat one," Kendrick said.

Landor frowned. "You have one and only one chance when it attacks. Its hide is thick and tough, and there are bony spikes that protrude from its neck and spine. Only its abdomen is soft enough to injure it quickly. The problem is that it stays low to the ground and will attack a man's legs first. The jaws are powerful enough to crush a man's bones. I am lucky to still have my leg."

Kendrick thought for moment. "How many will I face?"

"Only one…at a time," Landor said. "Each blood wolf marks its territory and will not venture beyond it. Two blood wolves in the same territory always fight to the death. While I was at the castle, ten wolves protected the boundaries. Lord Ra called them his pets." Landor seemed lost in thought and shook his head.

"What is it?" Kendrick asked.

"It's quite remarkable. Those beasts would devour any living creature, including each other…except Lord Ra. It was almost as if they knew he was even more vicious than they were. Lord Ra even named them."

Kendrick sucked in a deep breath. Landor's description of the blood wolves was helping him understand the mountain of evil he would soon face.

"When one beast would die or need to be replaced, the new beast would be given the name of the former. The beasts that protect the back of Lord Ra's castle at Bel Lione are Hypoc, Deceptor, Toxica, Revel, Plezior, and Arrogoy. On the eastern and western land are Destroyer, Carnage, Chaos, and Tormentor."

Kendrick thought for a long while. "How do I find the hidden entrance?"

Landor hesitated, then finally seemed to understand and yield to Kendrick's determination. As the planning continued, he responded with more enthusiasm. Gradually, in the process, two knights from opposite ends of the kingdom talked and became friends. It was a peculiar friendship forged by forces beyond the shores of Arrethtrae. It was not without tension, however, for Kendrick was always aware he was wagering his life on the knowledge and experience of one of Lord Ra's own knights.

The wager was great, but so was the stake—Duncan's life, and the lives of the youth of Bel Lione. Kendrick had no choice but to pursue it, and he would not be averted by blood wolves, Shadow Warriors, or even Lucius himself, for the power of the Prince was within him.

It was this power that lifted the words of the Code from its parchment and etched them on the fleshy tablets of Kendrick's heart—words that said, "Never abandon a fellow knight in battle or in peril!"

CHAPTER THIRTEEN

INTREPID
ENDEAVOR

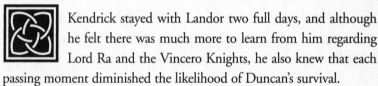Kendrick stayed with Landor two full days, and although he felt there was much more to learn from him regarding Lord Ra and the Vincero Knights, he also knew that each passing moment diminished the likelihood of Duncan's survival.

The parting with Landor stirred up a strange array of feelings in Kendrick—gratitude, for this former ally of Lord Ra had offered him hope for his fellow knight, and sadness, for he knew he would never see his new friend again. Even if Landor trusted Kendrick never to reveal his whereabouts, the risk was too great for him to remain in his cabin. Landor would once again disappear into the vastness that the kingdom of Arrethtrae offered, whether in the uninhabited regions of the land or the anonymity of the crowded cities.

The two men stood face to face at the ledge they had climbed together just two days earlier. The silence between them told Kendrick that something about his visit had changed Landor.

"Landor, I am grateful that our parting is made with both hearts beating." Kendrick offered his arm and a slight smile.

Landor responded with a nod and returned the gesture.

"Thank you for your help," Kendrick said. "I am indebted to you… my friend."

Landor met Kendrick's eyes but did not speak. The firm grip of his hand on Kendrick's forearm was enough.

Once they parted, Kendrick's concern for Duncan quickly over-whelmed every other concern. He hurried down the mountain and returned to the small farm where he had quartered Pilgrim, then spurred the horse in the direction of Bel Lione. As he rode, he mentally reviewed every piece of information Landor had given him. He felt within his vest a second time, checking to make sure the two maps were there—one defining the location of the secret entrance into Lord Ra's castle, and the other showing the labyrinth of tunnels and chambers within.

Kendrick arrived at Lionsgate by evening on his second day of travel. He considered initiating the rescue at once, but reason overruled desperation. The grounds surrounding Lord Ra's castle were extensive, and navigating north around them in the dark would be nearly impos-sible. He was also exhausted from his journey back to Bel Lione. He ate the meal Lady Odette and Elise had prepared, then allowed the strong arms of slumber to pull him into his bed.

Morning beckoned Kendrick from his sleep. He rose quickly and dressed in dark clothing. Over a hurried breakfast, he conveyed his in-tentions to Lady Odette and her children, then excused himself to the stable to make preparations. He had just secured Pilgrim's saddle when Ancel appeared in the doorway.

"Sir Kendrick…I…I…"

Kendrick turned to face him. "Ancel, everyone makes mistakes. The question is what do you do with the situation once you know it. Some men let their mistakes destroy them, but men of character embrace their mistakes and become stronger. The choice is yours and yours alone to make, but know that I don't condemn you. Neither does Duncan."

Ancel's gaze went to the ground and then back to Kendrick. "May I come with you?"

"No." Kendrick placed a hand on the boy's shoulder. "Your mother and your sister need a man of courage here." Ancel nodded. Kendrick watched him disappear through the stable's big front door.

"Thank you." Elise stood behind Kendrick. Her arms were folded, her countenance somber. "I heard what you told Ancel." She motioned with her head toward the door. "He's been brooding since you left."

"He's a good lad. He just needs a little confidence."

She nodded and didn't move. She looked as though she was about to weep. "Do you think Duncan is still alive?"

"If I didn't, I wouldn't have planned his rescue." He reached for his pack, trying to cover his own doubts with purposeful action.

Elise stepped closer, and a single tear fell down her cheek. "I'm so afraid—for Duncan…for you…for us all. Lord Ra is so powerful."

"Listen, his power is nothing compared to the King's." Kendrick finished strapping the pack behind the saddle and turned to face her. "Elise, the Knights of the Prince are taking back from Lucius all that belongs to the King. There is such great power in Him and in the Prince that Lord Ra trembles at the thought of it. That power is with Duncan, with me, and with all who believe in Him."

She studied him gravely. "I believe too. But please be careful." She stood on tiptoe and kissed Kendrick's cheek.

Kendrick smiled as he watched her leave. Elise was a beautiful young woman both inside and out, and Kendrick was glad she had chosen to give her heart to his young friend. Her love for Duncan solidified his resolve to face the day with courage.

He left the manor grounds astride Pilgrim, with Duncan's horse in tow, and found himself grateful for the cool breeze. He had purposely worn armor that would allow quick and quiet movements, but even light armor warmed up quickly in the bright sunshine.

Following Landor's recommendation, Kendrick journeyed north and then east, skirting the region under Lord Ra's direct influence. The castle of Bel Lione was off to his right, but much too far away to be seen.

He arrived at the northern foothills of Mount Quarnell by midafternoon and then turned southwest for a time. He climbed a knoll, from which he could just make out the rear towers of Lord Ra's castle in the distance.

According to Landor, this side of the castle was protected not only by the blood wolves but also by an outer wall that enclosed a bailey. The secret tunnel passed beneath this protective wall and outer yard and from there into the dungeon. Kendrick opened the map Landor had drawn for him and identified key terrain features to help him approximately locate the hidden entrance of the castle.

From this point on, Kendrick knew his senses must be on full alert, for he was entering the dark domain of the Shadow Warriors. The thought made his heart race, and he took several deep breaths to settle himself before folding the map and resuming his journey. He traveled much more slowly now and stopped often to check his location against the map.

After a while he spotted a jagged outcropping of rocks high above him and slightly to his left. Landor had called the formation Panther Peak, for its shape resembled the silhouette of a crouching panther. Kendrick made his way to the base of the peak and tied the horses there. He would cover the remaining distance on foot.

He found a clearing and stayed at its edge. The castle towers loomed much larger now, and his muscles tightened. According to his map, he would soon enter the territory of Lord Ra's blood wolves. He returned the map once more to his vest and drew his sword. Feeling the golden hilt in his hand was comforting, for the power of the Prince seemed to flow through it and into his arm.

Kendrick reached the far side of the clearing and moved on toward the castle. The hidden entrance would be another five hundred paces directly before him. He placed each foot carefully, feeling for twigs that might snap and announce his presence. With each step, Kendrick sensed the darkness of evil beginning to envelop him. It took great concentration not to let fear swell up within him. His sword grew heavy, and his lungs seemed to resist the air he was breathing. Two more steps, and Kendrick felt he was in the fog of a bad dream, where his legs were made of lead and each movement took great effort.

He stopped, listened, and looked behind him. His progress had been much slower than anticipated.

Where are those beasts? Dusk was approaching and before long he would be as blind as the monsters that awaited him. His sight was his only advantage. He chose to increase his pace.

He looked toward the castle. Through the half-bare trees he could now make out the dark form of the massive wall in the distance. A breeze rustled the dry leaves, and Kendrick didn't know if he was thankful for the sounds of the wind or not.

He moved forward another thirty paces and identified the two towers Landor had said would align when he was near the hidden entrance. Realizing he had veered slightly left, he turned to his right…and froze.

Just ten paces away, a mound of brown fur rose from a half burrow in the ground. A row of spiny horns on the creature's back stood up straight, and a demonic snarl filled the air.

Kendrick had tried to ready himself for this moment. But even with Landor's descriptions, nothing could have prepared him for the absolute terror that crouched before him. The blood wolf's sharp teeth glistened as it turned its head from side to side to pinpoint the location of its victim. Its milky, colorless eyes added to the impression that this monster was something more than a fierce animal. Its muscled haunches drew taut, and catlike talons dug into the soft soil in anticipation of its attack.

Kendrick swallowed hard, willing his mind to overcome the paralysis that seemed to grip his body. He slowly brought his left hand to the hilt of his sword and prepared for the blood wolf to attack low, as Landor had warned. But before Kendrick realized what was happening, the beast lunged straight for his throat. It attacked without taking a single step, covering the ten paces between them in a single leap.

It happened so quickly that Kendrick was unable to position his sword for the lethal blow to the beast's abdomen. Instead, he swung his sword with all his might and stepped back from the path of the flying beast.

"You have one and only one chance when it attacks." Landor's words resonated in Kendrick's mind as he sliced his sword across the blood wolf's thick hide. Could he possibly survive now that his one chance had come and gone?

He felt the edge of the blade penetrate until its upper portion hit the bony spikes of the beast's spine. The animal's bloodcurdling cry told Kendrick it was wounded, but it still managed to swipe with a claw as it passed, and the talons tore at his shoulder. His armor stayed secure, but the powerful blow spun Kendrick around like a doll made of rags and threw him to the ground.

He nearly lost his grip on the sword, but recovered and scrambled to a kneeling position just in time to see the blood wolf turn and attack again. This time it did not leap but ran low to the ground, straight for Kendrick.

For a moment, he didn't know what to do. He had no prior experience with this kind of enemy. And while he was grateful to have a second chance, he knew he wouldn't have another.

With only a split second remaining, Kendrick stayed on one knee and braced his right leg behind him. He took a modified hanging-guard stance by pulling the hilt of his sword near to the right side of his head and pointing its tip at the charging blood wolf.

The beast covered the last few steps to Kendrick at a frightening speed and opened its jaws to tear Kendrick's body to pieces. At that moment, he thrust forward with all of his might, aiming the tip of his sword at the blood wolf's open mouth. The blade penetrated the animal's throat, and the momentum of the beast's attack skewered it onto Kendrick's sword until the hilt was lodged against the blood wolf's teeth.

Kendrick stayed firmly planted until the massive body of the blood wolf slammed against him and sent him reeling backward. Pain shot through his body as he hit the ground with the animal's flailing body on top of him.

The death of the blood wolf was quick and silent. Kendrick pushed the carcass off of himself and lay panting on the ground, acutely aware of the stark pain in his right shoulder. He tried to move his arm, but any attempt brought unbearable pain. The joint was misaligned.

He let his head rest on the ground for a moment, looking for even the slightest relief and remembering what Landor had said about the blood wolf's territory. At least he wouldn't have to face more than one of those dreadful beasts.

After a few moments, Kendrick forced himself to stand. His right arm was useless; it felt like it had been nailed onto his shoulder backward. He couldn't continue in this condition, and yet he didn't dare turn back. Once the dead blood wolf was discovered, the castle guards would be alerted. A future rescue attempt would be impossible.

Kendrick searched until he found a tree with its roots exposed. Kneeling beside it, he grasped the root firmly with his right hand. He positioned his torso parallel to the ground and filled his lungs with air, then pulled steadily on his arm and began to rotate his shoulder.

The pain was excruciating, and he bit his lip to keep from screaming. When he couldn't bear it any longer, he released his grip and fell to the ground, wondering if his mission would be over before it had begun. He fought against the discouragement that settled into his heart as the pain in his shoulder spread to his whole body, rendering him useless. In his despair, his thoughts turned to the One who had suffered so much more than he.

My Prince, You have called me to this place…to this mission. One of Your knights is in peril under Lord Ra. Help me to help him, my King. Strengthen my heart that I might not fail You.

It took a fair while before he could muster the fortitude to make another attempt, but eventually he rose and set his face like flint. Once again he positioned himself above the thick root. This time he pulled harder and twisted his body further until he heard and felt his shoulder pop. Instantly the stabbing pain was replaced by a dull, constant ache that was at least bearable.

Kendrick returned to the dead blood wolf and knelt in front of it. His sword was still embedded in the animal's carcass. He had just placed his right hand on the hilt, wondering if there was enough strength left in his arm to remove it, when he heard the blood wolf growl.

Impossible! Kendrick jumped back, bewildered. Then he realized the growl had come not from this animal, but from somewhere behind him. He slowly turned to see another blood wolf, even larger than the one he'd slain, crouching just three paces away.

Kendrick's heart sank into his stomach, for he knew there was no escape.

The massive muscles of the blood wolf tightened in anticipation of the attack. It crouched for the lunge, fangs dripping. Then it froze, its head cocked to the left, ears lifted as if to listen. Kendrick took advantage of the pause and reached for his embedded sword, though he still believed the situation was all but hopeless.

Then Kendrick heard it too—the sound of air being split by a spear.

The blood wolf yelped as the spear sank deeply into its side. Kendrick pulled on his sword with all his might and carried the energy into a full swing that flew diagonally upward toward the blood wolf's neck. His sword hit the creature's shoulder in what should have been a death-blow, but the bony spines stopped the weapon short of its mark.

The injured wolf lunged for Kendrick. He rolled to the side at the last moment, barely avoiding the snapping jaws. Kendrick wondered how long it would take for the spear to kill it…and if he could last until then.

The blood wolf attacked again, and Kendrick could not bring his sword to bear in time. The powerful jaws of the beast crunched down on Kendrick's leg and would have severed it instantly were it not for his armor. Even with the protection, teeth pierced his flesh. Kendrick swung his sword at the blood wolf's neck but couldn't bring enough power for his slice to be effective.

The blood wolf released its grip on Kendrick's leg and lunged for his throat…just as a powerful sword tore into its body from above. Shrieking with anger and pain, it turned on its new attacker. But by the time it positioned itself, another slice from the man's sword had cut deeply into its throat. Blood spurted, and the beast collapsed.

Kendrick lay panting on the ground, stunned to discover he was still alive. He looked up, hardly believing what he saw.

"I thought you said they wouldn't cross into another's territory," Kendrick said between deep breaths.

Landor shrugged. "I guess I was wrong." He offered his hand to Kendrick and lifted him to his feet.

"To say that I am grateful is a bit of an understatement," Kendrick said.

"I'm just glad I arrived in time." Landor wiped the blood from his sword and slid it into his sheath with a businesslike snap. "We should be wary…if there were two, there could be more."

Kendrick nodded. He bent stiffly to retrieve his own weapon. "I didn't think I'd see you again, my friend."

Landor shook his head, as if he couldn't believe his own actions. "You are quite mad for doing this, and now I have become mad for helping you." He pointed past the blood wolf's carcass to a thick tangle of trees and bushes. "The entrance is just over there. Can you walk on that leg?"

Kendrick took a few steps. The pain from the blood wolf's bite caused him to limp slightly but didn't hinder him much. "I'll be all right. Let's go."

They made their way carefully to the overgrown area and felt for the stones that would indicate the entrance. Brush and vines had completely covered the depression leading to the door and the stone retaining wall. They cleared them away, then used a stone to break open the rusty lock that hung from the door's metal latch.

The thick wooden door creaked in resistance to the intrusion of its solitude. Kendrick saw Landor back up a step and wondered at his response. He looked at his older companion and recognized the face of fear.

"It's all right, Landor. I can go alone."

"No...you will need me. I just need a moment."

Kendrick took a cloth from his pouch and wrapped it tightly about a thick branch. He poured oil from a small flask onto the cloth and then used flint stone and the flat of his sword to light it. When the torch was ablaze and he was set, he looked at Landor. The older knight nodded, and the two allies from different realms entered into the belly of evil.

CHAPTER FOURTEEN

THE DUNGEONS OF LORD RA

Kendrick and Landor made their way down a dank tunnel that smelled of old roots. The darkness seemed to swallow the torchlight, so they could only see a few paces ahead and behind them, and the low ceiling prevented them from walking completely upright. In places, they had to step over rubble dislodged by tree roots, and from time to time a large rat would squeal and scurry away into the darkness ahead.

They traveled for some distance, until Kendrick supposed that they must be close to the castle wall. They came to a crude set of stairs that led farther down into the depths of the earth beneath the castle. The ground became damp and the air even more stale. Kendrick found it difficult to breathe, and the ache in his shoulder and leg seemed to worsen, but he tried to keep his mind focused on Duncan and not on his own misery.

At the bottom of the stairs, they stepped into ankle-deep muck that clung to their boots. Here the tunnel split to the left and to the right. Kendrick remembered this first junction on Landor's map but wanted to make sure of the direction.

"Which way do—," Kendrick turned to ask, but Landor motioned him to silence. "We are close to the dungeon now," he whispered. "Lord Ra's men may be near."

Landor pointed toward the left branch, and they traveled that direction until they reached a dead end. In the stone wall was a small recess, but there seemed to be no way forward.

Kendrick wondered if they had taken the wrong branch, but Landor put his ear to the wall and listened. After a long moment, he stepped away and took a deep breath, as if to prepare himself. Then he motioned for Kendrick to help him push against the right side of the wall.

At first it seemed as though they were pushing against a mountain, but they doubled their effort and the wall pivoted slightly. A sliver of dim light entered the tunnel, and Kendrick felt a rush of air. His torch flickered and threatened to go out.

The smell of this air was different—worse! It held the odors of human feces and death, and it frightened Kendrick. A deep moaning sound reached through the crack and warned them of what lay ahead.

They listened for any indication of discovery and then pushed on the wall again. This time it moved more easily, and they continued until the opening was wide enough for a man to slip through sideways. Kendrick extinguished his torch and placed it in another recess he'd discovered on the tunnel wall. Landor stepped through the large stone doorway, and Kendrick followed.

They stood side by side in an alcove off a dark passageway. As they looked around to get their bearings, a scream pierced the dungeon air and echoed off the stone walls. Cries and moans filtered through the passageways, some from men and some from women. Kendrick shuddered at the thought of anyone being held in the chambers here. This was a place of great woe.

"There are three levels to the dungeon," Landor whispered. "I think we are on the second. If your friend is still alive, he is probably in the torture chamber." Landor pointed downward. Kendrick's heart nearly despaired again, but he steeled himself.

"Take me there," he said to Landor.

They stepped cautiously from the cover of shadow and into the passageway. It stretched left and right, with many branches joined to it. An occasional torch in a bracket provided just enough light for them to see. Both men drew their swords and then ventured into a labyrinth of tunnels and chambers.

They passed countless captives in barred cells. Their faces were hollow, and their flesh hung from their frail bones like loose clothing. Some pleaded with them for help, but most just remained in a fetal position on the cold stone floor. Kendrick could hardly bear to look at them. His soul began to ache, and the discovery of this wretched place weighed heavy on his spirit.

They came to a corner, and Kendrick peered around it. He saw movement and heard heavy footsteps approach. He and Landor looked frantically for a place to hide, but there was none. They quickly backtracked a short distance and found a recessed area near a cell. They pressed their backs up against the stones near the cell's steel bars and waited.

The footsteps grew louder. Kendrick gripped his sword tightly, hoping he wouldn't have to use it just yet.

"Water…" came the plea of one of the captives. "Please…water…"

"Quiet, maggot!" came a hoarse shout. Kendrick peered from his hiding place to see a Shadow Warrior as large as those he had faced at the castle drawbridge about a week ago. The warrior kicked at the outstretched arms of the captive and cursed at him. He then turned toward another passageway, away from Kendrick and Landor. They waited a moment to be sure he was gone. Kendrick was just stepping back into the passageway when he felt five cold bony fingers grasp his arm. A rush of fear swept over his body.

"Please help me!" The plea was quiet but full of desperation. Kendrick turned to see the emaciated arm of a young woman reaching through the bars. Fear and pain filled her sunken eyes. Death was lurking near, and she knew it.

"I must go." Kendrick put his hand over hers. "But I will come back for you."

She just whimpered and clung to him more tightly.

"What is your name?" he asked.

She blinked. "I have not had a name for over six years, but I was once known as Teara."

"Come, Kendrick," Landor urged. "We must hurry!"

Kendrick gently squeezed her hand and then helped her release her grip. "I will come for you, Teara. I promise!" Kendrick looked once more into her eyes and vowed never to forget her image, for it was a picture of Lord Ra's work in the souls of men and women.

Landor led them through the maze to another staircase and then down to the third level. They took one wrong turn, backtracked, then had to avoid another guard before they came to a larger chamber filled with instruments and devices designed for purposes that Kendrick did not want to consider. This chamber stood empty, but the screams from an adjoining one echoed through the passageways.

"He is alive!" Kendrick said to Landor. A rising fury drove him toward the sound. He hurtled through a doorway to see a bleeding body stretched about a bloodstained wooden column. A hulking Shadow Warrior wielded a multistranded whip studded with metal fragments. Another warrior lounged against the far wall, laughing at the pain his cohort inflicted.

The warrior with the whip unleashed another swipe of torture onto the bloody back of his victim. Duncan screamed in agony as the whip lacerated his skin with new wounds.

Kendrick rushed upon them. *"No!"*

The two warriors were momentarily stunned, and Kendrick leapt to take advantage. Sword out, he lunged at the man who held the whip.

The warrior swiped the weapon at him, but Kendrick's righteous sword cut through the strands and penetrated deep into the torso of the sadistic warrior. He fell to the stone floor, his blood mixing with the blood of previous victims.

The other warrior drew his sword and came toward Kendrick with loathing in his eyes. Kendrick balanced himself and prepared for the impact. The swords engaged, and the sound of crashing steel echoed off the walls of Lord Ra's torture chambers.

"You will never make it out of here alive, fool!" snarled the massive Shadow Warrior.

"You are wrong, Guish," Landor said from behind him.

The warrior's head swiveled and he froze in confusion. Seconds later, his weapon clattered to the floor as Landor's and Kendrick's blades pierced his body. He fell to his knees with a look of astonishment across his scarred face.

"Landor…you…" The warrior grimaced, then fell to the floor dead.

Landor and Kendrick ran to release Duncan from his bonds. Kendrick caught him as he collapsed, lowering his friend gently to the floor and cradling his head and shoulders. Landor ran to the nearest passageway to look for more Shadow Warriors.

Duncan's body was torn from head to foot. He looked up at Kendrick, struggling to focus. "Kendrick," he whispered, "you came."

Kendrick fought back tears. Had he come this far only to watch his young companion die in his arms?

"Yes, Duncan, I came."

"I'm…so sorry…I…"

Kendrick stopped him. "There is nothing to be sorry for, Duncan. You risked your life to save Ancel. That kind of courage flows only from one who belongs to the Prince."

Duncan tried to smile through swollen, bleeding lips and then grimaced. "They'll be…coming soon," he said with great effort. "You must…leave me…"

"I'm not leaving without you." Kendrick shifted Duncan's weight in an effort to lift him, but Duncan grabbed his shoulder weakly.

"Take care of…Elise…," he whispered. Then his body went limp.

"Stay with me, Duncan!" Kendrick urged as Landor reappeared in the doorway.

"We have to get out of here fast!"

Kendrick nodded. "Help me carry him."

The two men lifted Duncan between them and headed back through the passageways. As of yet, there were no pursuing footsteps, but their progress felt much too slow. Duncan's weight was a challenge, especially when they came to the stairwell leading back up to the second level. Breathing hard, they made it back to the passageway near the secret exit before shouts of alarm began to echo down to them. They increased their pace, but the sound of boots running on stone floors grew louder with each passing second.

With every step, Kendrick felt exhaustion close in. Sweat poured down his face and the pain in his leg and shoulder triggered waves of nausea. Kendrick stole a glance at Landor and saw the older man was near the limit of his physical ability.

The entrance was just ahead. They half carried, half dragged Duncan toward it as the shouts and footsteps grew louder behind them. Neither of the men could talk, nor did they try. The commotion from the captives in the cells rose in volume. Chaos seemed to fill the dungeon, spreading throughout all three levels. Kendrick assumed their pursuers didn't know exactly where to search. If they did, they surely would have found them by now.

They reached the alcove, and Landor slipped through the opening first. It took some maneuvering to get Duncan through, but Landor finally dragged him clear so Kendrick could pass through. They both grabbed the recess on the other side of the stone door and pulled to close it, but there was not enough area for them to get a firm grip and pull the massive door inward.

Kendrick looked about for some other way to pull the wall closed. He found a place on the wall to set his foot against for leverage, and the two men pulled on the wall with all of their might. Slowly it began to move, and the sliver of light streaming in narrowed. They worked the door two more times before the wall finally came to rest in its original position.

Kendrick and Landor slid down the walls opposite one another until they rested on the moist, cool ground, their energy spent. Even through their heavy breathing, they heard the faint sounds of a frenzied search being conducted just a few feet away.

After a few moments, Kendrick crawled over to Duncan, wondering if their rescue had been in vain. He laid his head on Duncan's chest and detected a faint heartbeat, then rolled over on his back, weak with gratitude and relief.

Landor made his way to Kendrick in the dark. "We cannot linger long. Their search will expand, and soon they will discover the dead blood wolves. We must bury them and erase any evidence of our presence."

"Yes, I agree." Kendrick had to reach deep for the strength to stand.

They relit their torch, lifted Duncan once more, and began the slow, painful journey back from Lord Ra's chambers of torture and death. Kendrick found himself haunted by what he had seen beneath the stronghold of that evil Shadow Warrior. In his mind he heard the moans of the captives and saw the dry-eyed despair on the face of an emaciated girl. The compassion of the Prince filled his heart and solidified his resolve.

He turned his gaze back to the castle before they mounted their steeds.

I'll not forget, Teara, he vowed. *I will come for you!* 🔲

CHAPTER FIFTEEN

I WILL CONQUER

 They journeyed far enough to be safely out of Lord Ra's immediate searches, setting up camp in the northern foot-hills of Mount Quarnell. In spite of his exhaustion, Kendrick bandaged up Duncan as best he could and tended him throughout the night.

Duncan drifted in and out of consciousness as he fought for his very life. Kendrick watched him, wrestling with the decision of whether to travel or not. Lady Odette and Elise would be better equipped to nurse Duncan to health. But getting him there—a full day's undertaking—could kill him.

By midmorning of the next day, Kendrick realized he had no choice. Duncan's wounds needed fresh bandages, and fever would set in if he wasn't properly cared for. Kendrick and Landor laid Duncan on his horse and secured him once more on the animal's back. By late evening, they arrived at Lady Odette's manor.

Elise was the first to meet them. "Duncan!" she screamed. Lady Odette and Ancel came running.

"We must get him to a bed and change his bandages quickly." Kendrick dismounted and began to pull Duncan off his horse. Landor helped. Introductions could wait.

Elise wept when she saw Duncan's swollen face and the hundreds of gashes across his body. She didn't seem to know what to do with herself. She reached out to touch him, then pulled back her hand, her face reflecting the excruciating pain of his wounds. Ancel put an arm about her and walked beside her as Kendrick and Landor carried Duncan into the manor.

"Take him to his room," Lady Odette began calling out orders with the confidence of a general commanding an army. Her confidence brought no small relief to Kendrick. He knew that if Duncan could be saved, Lady Odette would do it. Elise seemed to emerge from her shock as she applied herself to the nursing duties her mother had assigned to her.

Once Kendrick and Landor had exhausted their usefulness to Lady Odette, they each fell asleep in their beds. Kendrick awoke to find afternoon sun streaming through the window. His leg and shoulder ached, but he rose and hurried to Duncan's bedside. Elise was there, looking as if she had never left. Her hand lay gently over Duncan's.

Kendrick didn't say a word. He walked to the opposite side of the bed, relieved to see Duncan's chest rising and falling peacefully. Elise looked up at him, and he saw the weariness of angst upon her face. As she gazed into Kendrick's eyes, her own filled with tears.

"Thank you for what you've done," she said. "You are a brave knight."

Kendrick nodded toward Duncan. "He would have done the same for me."

"Yes," she replied, her voice tender. "Yes, he would have."

Kendrick left Elise to continue her care for Duncan. He stopped in the kitchen, where Lady Odette had left food for him, then went to seek out Landor.

He found him sitting beneath a large oak tree a fair distance from the manor, near a stone wall that bordered the estate. The late-autumn air was brisk but refreshing, the air filled with birdsong. Kendrick wondered if Landor was enjoying the reprieve from the icy world of his mountain refuge.

He walked over and leaned against the wall. "I wish I could find words to express my gratitude, Landor."

Landor's gaze seemed to be off to a distant world, or perhaps a distant past.

"He's fortunate to be alive...as are we," Landor said. "Lord Ra will be furious. I still don't understand..." He shook his head.

"Understand what?"

"No one has ever escaped from Lord Ra. I truly didn't think it was possible."

"That's because you have not known the Prince," Kendrick said. "With Him, all things are possible."

Landor flashed a smile. "Ah, yes...your Prince." He pushed to his feet and went to join Kendrick at the stone wall. "Well, He certainly has power over *you*."

Now it was Kendrick's turn to smile. A moment of silence passed between them, and Kendrick's thoughts turned to the dungeons of Ra's castle and the prisoners there. "Tell me, Landor...what exactly did I see in those dungeons? Who are those prisoners?"

Landor looked to the ground for a moment and then back to Kendrick. "Lord Ra is here to bring chaos and ruin to the kingdom of Arrethtrae. The festivals of Bel Lione were created to lure the youth of this region into his realm of influence."

"That much I know."

"But what you don't know is that everyone who participates is changed. A young person will typically respond in one of three ways to the pleasures and indulgences offered by Ra."

He paused again. Kendrick waited. Landor finally went on, "The first response is to be caught up in the frivolous, carefree activities for a while. Young people who react this way may grow discontented with the world outside Lord Ra's castle and resist the rules and counsel of their parents, and this sows seeds of discord in families that can last for many years. But eventually they do decide to leave the castle and go back into the world. They find a craft or trade to support themselves, get married, and start their families. But then they become feeders for Ra. They will actually encourage their children to enjoy the pleasures of youth for a season, not fully comprehending how closely they came to complete and utter destruction. This is the response of most people who attend the festivals.

Kendrick raised an eyebrow. "And the second?"

"The second response is for young people to be so completely taken with the activities at the castle that they can think of nothing else. They live for each weekly fete and monthly festival, thinking daily of the enticements Ra offers, especially the rich food, strong drink, and other pleasures. It may take weeks or months or even years, but eventually these young people reach the point where they abandon their life outside the castle walls and accept Ra's offer to actually live in the castle. What they don't realize is that once they make this decision, they can never leave, even if they want to." Landor gave Kendrick a dark look. "Never!"

"The prisoners?" Kendrick asked.

"Yes. They grow weak from the indulgences. Then one day they are taken to the dungeons, where Lord Ra and his Shadow Warriors take great pleasure in their torment and hopelessness. There are fewer people who respond this way. But as you could see by the cells, many do eventually fall into the snare of death that Ra has set for them."

Landor fell silent and seemed to forget Kendrick was even there.

"Landor?" Kendrick finally asked.

The other man turned slowly and stared at Kendrick. The glint of darkness in his eyes reminded Kendrick of what he had seen in the cabin, when Landor revealed himself as a Vincero Knight.

Kendrick's brow furrowed. "And the third?"

Landor's gaze softened slightly, and he took a deep breath. "The third response is one that only few people have. Ra closely watches all who enter into his festivals, looking for just the right ones." Landor paused again and seemed to find it difficult to go on. "These young people enjoy the sensual pleasures Lord Ra offers. But instead of growing weaker from indulgence, they grow harder and more depraved. These are the youth who thrive on the violent sporting games, finding their pleasure in the violence of the games and the torment of the wild pigs used in the contests. This is what Lord Ra wants...for they are his recruits."

"I've been told that parents want this too—to have their sons and daughters serve in Lord Ra's castle."

Landor curled a lip. "If only they knew what that means. Lord Ra takes the very best—or perhaps more accurately the very worst—and trains them to master the sword. He equips them with an entire armory of evil plots and devices and sets them loose to wreak destruction and chaos upon the region. He promises them great power and prestige. He calls them conquerors."

Landor's tone grew ominous. "In reality, Lord Ra owns their souls and takes great pleasure in watching his reach expand through the death and destruction they cause. These men and women become—" Landor broke off and turned away from Kendrick.

Kendrick finished softly, "The Vincero Knights."

Landor nodded.

Kendrick pondered what Landor had just told him and wondered how such a thing could happen. Surely there must be many who chose to be willfully ignorant of Lord Ra's plots.

Landor turned back to face Kendrick. "In the mountains you said Ra and his warriors were more than mere Arrethtraen men. You called them Shadow Warriors. I can see that now. I've heard of other strongholds in the kingdom that train Vincero Knights too. If the Dark Knight truly controls all of them, then he must be powerful indeed!"

"Yes," Kendrick replied. "But his days are numbered. One day he will face the Prince, and it will be his end." Kendrick's thoughts turned back to Teara. "Do all of Ra's guards and knights know of the prisoners he keeps in the dungeons?"

Landor shook his head. "No. There are two guardhouses—one for Ra's Shadow Warriors, where the access to the dungeon is, and one on the other side of the castle yard for his Arrethtraen guards and knights."

"You're saying the Arrethtraen recruits don't know anything?"

"Some of them may suspect, but they learn quickly not to ask questions and not to go into the warrior guardhouse. When a youth is taken captive, it is done at such a time and in such a way that no one sees it."

Landor's voice dropped only to a whisper. "Only those who become Vincero Knights learn the full truth of the dungeons."

"And you were such a one?" Kendrick tried to imagine Landor as a bloodthirsty knight whose sole purpose was to destroy, but all he could see was a man who risked his life to save his own and Duncan's. It didn't make any sense. "Why did you leave?" Kendrick asked.

Landor walked over to the tree, placed his hand on its thick trunk, and leaned against it. He lowered his head and Kendrick could tell he was struggling with something deep.

"I was one of Lord Ra's loyal Vincero Knights. For years I did his bidding and destroyed many people...many homes...many dreams. I gathered a band of murderous thieves to broaden my influence, much as Lord Ra has done, and to insulate me from the crimes. Then one day something snapped inside me and I...I couldn't..."

Landor swallowed hard. He straightened and turned to face Kendrick. "I couldn't do it anymore. That day I mounted my horse and rode. I rode until night fell and then rode the next day too, caring not what direction I took or where I ended up. When I stopped, I hid, because I knew that once you belonged to Lord Ra, you always belonged to him. I knew he would come for me, and he did—over and over and over. He sent other Vincero Knights after me—at first to bring me back, later to kill me. I have been running and hiding for many years."

Landor's voice grew heavy with weariness. "I am tired. When you came to me, I…well, I found it impossible to refuse you." He looked straight into Kendrick's eyes and smiled sadly. "Your heart seemed so pure, even after having endured your own tragedy. I found myself curiously refreshed by your goodness. I…wanted more. And now…" He paused, a look of bafflement on his face.

Kendrick walked over to Landor and placed a hand on his shoulder. "I am neither pure nor good, Landor, and it is not me you seek. What you see in me is the work of the Prince, for only He is pure and good. He has called all who are weary and heavy laden, my friend. Through Him you will find rest. He came to restore this land, these people"— Kendrick swept his hand as if to include the whole region—"and to restore you, no matter what you've done. He came also to destroy the strongholds Lucius has built and to free those who are in bondage!" Kendrick stood tall and faced his new friend. "That is why I'm going back."

Landor looked at Kendrick in disbelief. "To Ra's castle?"

Kendrick nodded. "Lord Ra and the castle of Bel Lione must be destroyed and his captives set free."

"My friend," Landor said quietly. "We overcame those two warriors because of surprise, not because of our might. Ra commands an army of guards, knights, and warriors that strikes terror into the hearts of all. Men don't fight him; they flee from him. You still don't understand his power!"

Kendrick shook his head. "No, Landor. *You* still don't understand the *Prince!* Tomorrow I ride for Chessington to call all Knights of the Prince to arms against Lord Ra. Ride with me and see what great and mighty things the King and His Son are doing in the hearts of men and women across the land. It is time to retake this region, not hide in fear."

Landor looked at Kendrick and did not scoff at him this time. Something in Kendrick's passion seemed to crack the wall that he had built around his heart…something powerful. ▩

CHAPTER SIXTEEN

CALL TO COURAGE!

 The following morning, Kendrick rose and began his preparations for the journey back to Chessington. He went to the stable to saddle Pilgrim and found Landor packing his own steed.

"Going somewhere, Sir Landor?" Kendrick asked.

Landor chuckled. "It turns out that a certain madman has invited me on a journey. I am found with some time on my hands and thought I might join him."

Kendrick laughed and slapped his friend on the back. "I can promise you one thing. When you say yes to the Prince, you had better hang on tight, for His stallion rides far and fast!"

The two men finished packing their mounts and went together to see Duncan. Elise was smiling when they entered the room. Duncan turned his head and opened his eyes.

"You're awake," Kendrick said, crossing over to the bedside.

The young man raised his forearm off the bed to reach for Kendrick, who carefully took his hand.

"I owe you my life, Kendrick," Duncan said.

Kendrick thought he still looked like he had just been dragged behind a horse, but he was elated to see him awake and talking. "We've been worried about you, my young friend."

"I am well taken care of." Duncan managed something like a smile on his swollen face. He motioned with his eyes to Elise without turning his head.

Kendrick looked to Elise, who was wiping a tear away from her eye. "Yes. You are well taken care of."

"You look like you are on a mission." Duncan made an attempt to look past Kendrick to Landor, who still stood in the doorway.

Kendrick motioned for Landor to come closer. "Duncan, meet the man who truly saved your life...and mine. Sir Landor."

Landor shook his head as if contradicting the statement, but Duncan held out a hand to him.

"Sir Landor, I am truly grateful. Your courage and nobility is something I shall aspire to."

Landor seemed challenged as to how to respond. He just nodded.

"Duncan," Kendrick said. "Landor and I are about to leave for Chessington to meet with the council. I go to call the Knights of the Prince to ride against Lord Ra and his castle."

Duncan's eyes widened and he tried to sit up, grimacing with each movement. Kendrick and Elise put their hands to his shoulders.

"Duncan, what are you doing?" Kendrick asked.

"I must come with you...this is too important...please!" Duncan pleaded.

Kendrick put on a stern face. "You're in no condition to make this journey. Lie down, rest, and heal. It will be many days before I can gather a large enough force to attack Ra. If you have recovered by the time I return, you can join us."

Duncan had no more energy to argue. He settled back to his bed and closed his eyes. He nodded once. "The King reigns!" he said as he grabbed Kendrick's hand again.

"And His Son!" Kendrick replied, gripping Duncan's hand as a farewell.

Elise followed the two men out of the room.

Kendrick put a gentle hand on her shoulder. "Take care of him…if you can."

"I shall try." She smiled up at Kendrick. "He is strong. If I can keep him resting, I am certain he will recover quickly." She gave Kendrick a quick hug. "May the Prince be with you."

Kendrick gently hugged her back. "And with you."

Despite his concern for Duncan and eagerness to ride against Lord Ra, Kendrick enjoyed the six-day journey to Chessington with Landor. They spent some time riding in companionable silence and some time talking. Kendrick found himself growing quite fond of the older gentleman. When their discourse offered Kendrick an opportunity, he gently turned the conversation to the Prince—the mighty works He had done and was doing in the kingdom. Landor listened carefully but made few comments, and Kendrick was not inclined to push.

When they arrived at Chessington, a special council meeting was called. Kendrick relayed all the past events and his discoveries to William and the rest of the council, who voted unanimously to provide Kendrick with as much support as possible. A call immediately went out from Chessington for all Knights of the Prince who were able to join forces with Kendrick against Lord Ra and the castle of Bel Lione.

All through the following week, many men and women arrived to join Kendrick. They came not for fame, not for fortune, not for power, but for love of the Prince. Landor was amazed at how this loyalty transcended boundaries of family, class, dialect, and region. By week's end, more than five hundred knights had gathered to journey with Kendrick back to Bel Lione or had sent word that they would meet him there.

Fearing that such a large force would draw too much attention from Lord Ra, the council heeded Landor's suggestion to divide into smaller teams. No more than five knights would travel together in a group, to arrive at different times from different directions. The thickly forested region far north of Bel Lione was chosen as an encampment site, for they could make their way closest to the castle gate unseen from that direction.

Over the course of the next five days, the Knights of the Prince departed Chessington and traveled north over multiple routes. Kendrick and Landor were among the last to leave and so arrived back at Lionsgate nearly four weeks after they'd left there. Duncan greeted them in the courtyard with his sword on his belt and a broad smile upon his face.

"I thought you'd never get here," he said. "Were you successful?"

"Yes," Kendrick replied.

Landor shook his head, frowning. "It is not enough. Lord Ra will have nearly one thousand guards, knights, and Shadow Warriors within the castle, and who knows how many Vinceros."

"It will have to be enough," Kendrick said, refusing to be discouraged. "How are you feeling, Duncan?"

"Fit and ready for battle." He placed his hand on the hilt of his sword.

Kendrick looked him over. He wasn't entirely convinced.

"You couldn't keep me from this battle if you tried," Duncan added defiantly.

"No. I don't suppose I could." Kendrick put a hand to his young friend's shoulder. "Come, let's talk."

Most of the volunteer force was already in place by the time Kendrick, Duncan, and Landor arrived at the encampment north of Bel Lione.

The three knights then spent many hours in the campaign tent with the five captains who had been selected to help lead the force, relating all they knew about Ra and the castle and carefully plotting their assault.

"We must gain entrance to the castle before there is any discovery of an attack," Landor insisted, and many knights nodded in agreement. "If they manage to drop the gates and raise the drawbridge, your battle will end before it begins."

Landor unrolled a rough plan of the castle that he and Duncan had managed to sketch out. The knights were gathered around a table, searching the map for any possible weakness.

"I agree with Landor," Kendrick said. "Laying siege to the castle is not an option. They would surely outlast us, and who knows what would happen to the prisoners. With our numbers, it is paramount we gain access to the castle secretly."

"From what you have told us, getting even one knight into the castle undetected seems impossible," a knight named Winston said. "How in the kingdom are we to get five hundred?"

Silence followed his question. No one had an answer.

"These woods come close to the drawbridge," Duncan offered, pointing to an area northwest of the castle gate. "Perhaps if we rush upon them from the edge of the woods, they will not have enough time to secure the castle."

Landor shook his head. "You must all understand that Lord Ra's spies are everywhere. He knows almost everything that happens in this region. Although we are far away, I'd be surprised if he doesn't already know we are here. It would take a miracle to bring a force of five hundred to the edge of his castle without his knowledge."

"Would a diversion of some sort help?" asked another knight.

"What did you have in mind?" Kendrick asked in return.

"You said that youth are let in for the monthly festivals and the weekly fetes. Could we get one of them to do something from within?"

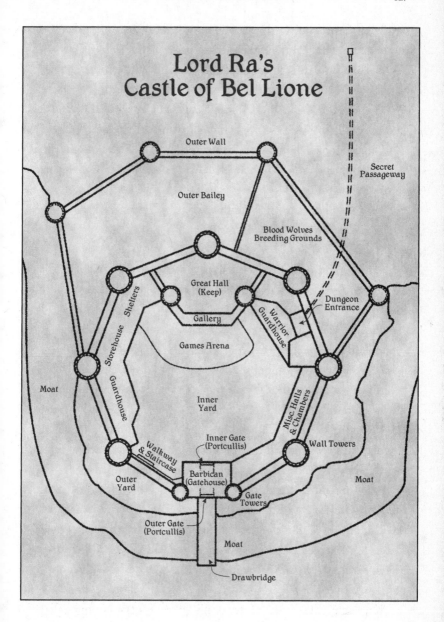

Lord Ra's
Castle of Bel Lione

"Yes!" Duncan said. "There are a number of thatched wooden shelters near the games court. If those could be set aflame…"

A murmur of approval ran around the table. Fire within a castle is always a great concern, for there is much to burn and little to stop it.

"Yes," Landor said. "But Duncan has already proven that Ra and his warriors can identify even a young knight with relative ease."

Duncan took a deep breath, knowing Landor spoke the truth. Even before Casimir identified him at the festival, the Shadow Warriors had been watching him.

"We would have to ask a youth to do it," Winston said. "One who is no apparent threat to Ra and his warriors."

"I'll do it."

With those words, the back wall of the tent lifted up. Eight knights reached for their swords, then replaced them when they recognized the speaker was but a lad of sixteen.

"Ancel," Kendrick said fiercely, "what are you doing here?"

"I'll do it!" Ancel repeated.

"How long have you been listening, son?" Winston asked.

Ancel stood straighter. "Long enough to know you need me to set fire to the castle."

Winston exited the tent, and the men inside heard him rebuke the knights who were supposed to be standing watch over their encampment. Extra knights were assigned, and he quickly returned.

Ancel turned to Kendrick. "Please, sir. I was foolish, and I caused Duncan—and you—great harm. Now I am certain Lord Ra was behind the death of my father, and he has brought great pain to many in Bel Lione. I've watched my friends change, and one of them even disappeared because of him. Let me join you and help destroy this monster. I am not afraid!"

Kendrick looked to the faces of his fellow leaders. No one offered any objection. It was the only plan thus far that had any credence.

"I will discuss it with your mother," he told the boy. "The decision will be hers."

Ancel nodded, and the rest of the knights seemed encouraged.

"We still need to secure the gate and drawbridge before we reveal our force," Winston said. "This diversion will help us do that, but how do we take advantage of it?"

The men returned their attention to the map on the table.

"There is only one option," Kendrick said as he stroked his short beard. He pointed to a place on the northeast grounds beyond the castle wall. Landor slowly nodded his head in agreement.

"What is there?" a captain asked.

"It's the secret passageway Landor and I took to rescue Duncan," Kendrick said. "If we are fortunate, they may not have discovered it yet. We were careful to cover our tracks."

"But it leads to the second level of the dungeons," Duncan said. "That is a fair distance from the front gate. A force coming in that way would surely be detected before they reached the gate."

Most of the knights nodded. "It seems impossible," one of them said.

"There is a way," Landor replied.

He threw a metal disk onto the map. It spun about, oscillating in its circular fall until it came to rest directly over the gate of the castle.

It was the medallion of a Vincero Knight.

The stunned captains glared at him with suspicion in their gaze.

"Be at peace, gentlemen," Kendrick said. "Landor was indeed a Vincero Knight. But he has risked his life twice for us, and I am proud to call him my friend. You have my word you can trust him." Kendrick locked eyes with Landor across the table. "I do."

Silence hung in the room for a long moment as the knights exchanged glances, then reached an unspoken agreement.

Winston nodded to Landor. "What do you propose?"

"I will enter the dungeons as a Vincero Knight escorting three prisoners to their cells. This is not unusual." Landor pointed to the map as if he could see the events unfolding beneath his finger. "We will make our way to the castle gate and secure it while Ancel's fire is burning. Then the rest of the force will enter through the gate, and your battle will begin."

"It is too dangerous," Kendrick said. "Ra is still looking for you, and if you are discovered—"

Landor cut him off. "It is the only way."

"And I will go with Landor," Duncan added.

"No—" Kendrick protested, but Duncan interrupted.

"Kendrick, I am the only other one who has seen the dungeons and knows the layout. Landor will need me. There is no other choice."

Kendrick wrestled with the logic of the suggestion and then finally yielded. He slowly nodded, and the other knights agreed.

"So be it. Find two more volunteers," he said to the captains. "They must be young or at least look young."

"One of the female knights would make our ruse even more believable," Landor added.

The men discussed a few more details of the mission and agreed the assault would begin on the following evening, in conjunction with the weekly fete. After all was finished, they adjourned. Duncan went with the captains to find two more volunteers for their mission, but Landor stayed behind with Kendrick. His words were solemn.

"Even if all goes according to plan—which I have my doubts about since we have hinged our whole operation on the success of a boy—you still don't have enough men to defeat Ra and his warriors. I fear you are leading them all to a slaughter."

Kendrick considered Landor's words carefully. He laid a hand on his shoulder. "My friend, I find myself more and more indebted to you with each passing day, for you have sacrificed much and risked even more on my behalf. Your wisdom and logic have become my greatest ally, and I want you to know I take your warning very seriously. But you must understand we are doing more here than storming a castle. We are fighting to bring hope to a land that does not understand it, for they do not understand the Prince. It is my hope that one day you yourself will come to believe in Him."

Kendrick looked deep into Landor's eyes and could see the desire but not the evidence. Landor put his hand on Kendrick's.

"You have shown me many wonderful things that would testify to the existence of this man you call the Prince, but the greatest of them all is your heart."

Kendrick nodded and accepted the honor of his words. They prepared to leave, but Landor looked once again at Kendrick.

"I must admit that your Prince is no longer a fairy tale to me."

Kendrick responded with a smile. "It's a start."

Later Kendrick took Ancel back to Lady Odette and shared the events of the evening with her. Ancel was quiet as Kendrick described the plan for entering the castle. He didn't implore her to agree, for his own heart could hardly justify the danger the boy would be in.

"Once the battle begins," she asked, her brow furrowed, "how can I be sure of his safety?"

Kendrick considered carefully before answering. "My lady, I can assure you of nothing. But I can promise that I will do my utmost to protect him once we are inside the castle."

They both looked toward Ancel, and he tried to appear older and stronger than he was. "I can do it, Mother... I know I can."

Kendrick said nothing more, but left Lady Odette to assimilate the information and weigh the cost. He didn't have to explain the significance of Ancel's role to their success. She understood at once, though her efficient mind and call to duty were clearly at odds with her heart as a mother.

They retired for the evening, and by morning Lady Odette had made her decision.

Kendrick then rode back to his men and began to prepare them for battle…a battle that would shake the very heart of the kingdom.

By late the next afternoon, all of the battle preparations were complete. Landor, Duncan, and two other young knights had departed hours earlier to circle the castle and enter the secret passageway. Orders had been given, and various groups had taken their positions. Kendrick had assigned Sir Winston to be his vice commander, for the man had already won the respect of those prepared to fight.

Now all that was left was the waiting. Kendrick walked among the brave souls who had come to join him in battle against this evil foe. He talked with them and wanted to remember each face and voice. They were all mighty in his eyes, for they came to sacrifice without compensation. But was he a worthy man to lead them?

"Sir Winston," he said, "see to the needs of the knights, will you? I need some time."

"Yes sir," Winston replied.

Kendrick mounted Pilgrim and rode deeper into the woods until he could no longer hear the sounds of the encampment. In the perfect stillness of the forest, Kendrick momentarily allowed himself the emotions that his men did not want to see.

He dismounted and walked a short distance, allowing his steed to follow on a loose rein. For the first time in many months, he felt weary. His armor felt heavy, and he labored to take each step. He stopped and began to wonder if his passion had brought him to a place he shouldn't be. He drew his sword, set its tip into the ground, and knelt before it. His eyes drank in the streams of winter sunlight gliding in between the bare tree limbs.

Kendrick lowered his eyes and fought the feelings of fear, doubt, and apprehension. In his silent contemplation, Kendrick searched for the foundation upon which his life had been renewed…no, reborn.

"My Prince, who am I that You should incline Your ears to my words or lift Your hand to my aid? I am not worthy to serve, and yet You chose me for this day. Help us defeat this great enemy of Yours that men might be free to believe in You."

"Sir Kendrick." The sound of a soft, deep voice landed upon his ears, and he was startled. He looked up to see a massive warrior standing a few paces before him in full battle regalia. The bright and polished sword at his side nearly glowed, and his countenance was even fiercer than before.

Kendrick stood and faced Bronwyn.

"The Prince has been with you from the beginning," the Silent Warrior told him. "As I and my brethren will be with you now."

Kendrick instantly felt his strength return, and his heart was warmed by the fire of the Prince. "How many of you will there be?"

"Enough." Bronwyn stepped forward until he was an arm's length away from Kendrick. "You must secure the castle gate, and then we will come." He looked deep into Kendrick's eyes. "I've waited many years, Kendrick. Go now in courage and know that the King reigns."

"And His Son!" Kendrick returned.

The two men exchanged a look of bonded unity that only those entering battle side by side could feel. Then they parted.

Kendrick returned to the encampment and gathered the knights into one place. He stood on raised ground so he could see all of them.

"Fellow Knights of the Prince, we do not face only Arrethtraen men of flesh and blood. We have come to battle against powers and rulers of darkness in high places. Lord Ra of Bel Lione is an evil and wicked Shadow Warrior, and today we stand against him! Though we carry the hope of the Prince to the people of Arrethtrae, we also bring to bear all the power of the King and His Son against Lucius and his evil Shadow Warriors, so that our fellow countrymen might be free from this bondage. Today, comrades, we will destroy this stronghold, for greater is the Prince within our hearts than all the forces of darkness against which we fight!"

Kendrick felt the passion of the Prince within his being as he drew his sword and held it high above him. "Put on your full armor and rise up with me to battle, for the King reigns!"

"And His Son!" shouted the other five hundred knights in unison, and they lifted their swords with one accord to affirm their resolution.

They rode toward the castle in silence and arrived as the weekly fete began. At the edge of the forest they waited—waited for the success of a boy and a former Vincero Knight. ▧

CHAPTER SEVENTEEN

INTO THE CASTLE

Duncan, Landor, and their two comrades reached the secret passageway with time to spare. They entered its dark and murky walls without encountering blood wolves or Shadow Warriors. The ease of their progress made Landor nervous, but they still continued through the tunnel, holding their torches before them.

As they neared the entrance into the dungeon, Duncan found it difficult to quell the fear and anxiety rising within him. Just weeks before, he had been a victim of the torture chambers beyond the stone doorway. Even now, the pain of those days had not completely left him. But something about him had changed. He made a deliberate decision to embrace the pain, to let it make him stronger as he focused on the countless men and women who were still in the dungeons and would die there if he faltered.

"Give me your swords, and I will carry them at my back in my belt," Landor whispered when they came to the stone door at the end of the tunnel. "My cloak should amply cover them while we are in the dungeon, for there is very little light."

The dancing light of their torches randomly illuminated various features of Landor's face as he spoke. His white beard was gone, and he looked ten years younger than before. Having donned the cloak and colors of the Vincero Knights, he presented a convincing facade, so much so that Duncan had to resist the urge to deny him his sword.

"Once inside," he added, "you must walk in single file before me. Duncan, you lead. Then Gregory, and then Kinley."

Duncan's fellow knights gathered closer to listen to his orders. Gregory was a little shorter than Duncan but with a similar build. His hair was brown and wavy. He was actually Duncan's age but looked younger. Kinley was a plain young woman, but her eyes were not; beneath her straight black bangs, they flashed with a knight's courage and passion. Duncan greatly admired her courage in volunteering for such a dangerous mission. She swiped a portion of her bangs that hung across her eyes and tucked it behind her ear as Landor spoke.

"What you are about to see will appall you," Landor told them soberly. "Don't be concerned about hiding your shock, for it will only make you all the more believable. You just—"

Duncan held up both hands to silence his comrades.

"Did you hear that?" he whispered, peering back up the tunnel through which they had come, his muscles suddenly rigid with fear. The others listened intently, barely breathing. Seconds passed. Finally they heard a deep moan, but its source was on the opposite side of the stone door and not from the tunnel behind them.

"We have no choice," Landor said. "We must go now."

Duncan steeled himself, and he saw each of his companions do the same. Landor took a deep breath as he turned to enter Bel Lione's dungeon of despair once more. They forced the stone door open, extinguished their torches, and entered the dungeon.

The putrid smell of death filled Duncan's nostrils, and he could not repress the flood of nightmarish memories that surfaced in response. He felt naked without his sword, and he wondered if the other two felt the same. Landor drew his sword, and Duncan led the other two "prisoners" down the first corridor, passing cell after cell of imprisoned souls.

Landor commanded turn after turn and finally brought them to the stairwell leading up to the first level.

Here Duncan became uneasy. He was sure Landor felt the same way. Prisoners were always taken *down* the three levels of the dungeon, never *up*, so if they met a guard at this point, all might be revealed.

Duncan took two steps up. "Down from the stairs, knave!" he heard Landor shout.

Duncan turned just as Landor shoved the other two against the stone wall and lunged toward him. He grabbed Duncan's shirt and yanked him backward so that he stumbled and fell to the floor with a thud.

Anger battled with terror and confusion as Duncan scrambled to his knees. Was Landor playing the double ruse and manifesting his true self as a Vincero Knight once more? Duncan tried to stand, but Landor struck him across the head with the pommel of his sword.

"Fool!" he shouted. "You chose to trust me, and now you will spend the rest of your pitiful life in these cells." He said the words with such loathing that Duncan was convinced they had been betrayed. He put his hand to his head, expecting to feel the warm trickle of his blood between his fingers, but there was none.

"Bring him to the chambers when you are done with him," Duncan heard a raspy voice say. "I'll give him torment he'll never forget!"

Duncan turned and saw a huge Shadow Warrior walking past them. The warrior's guttural laughter reverberated off the walls, and Duncan realized what was happening.

"I don't belong here," he pleaded, following Landor's lead. "Please let me go home!"

"Quiet!" Landor lifted the sword to strike him again. Now Duncan noticed that Landor's hand covered the pommel of his sword. This explained the lack of blood and the absence of any real pain.

Once the Shadow Warrior turned from the corridor, Landor reached for Duncan's hand and lifted him up.

"That was too close," he said. "Quickly!"

He motioned toward the stairwell, and they ascended to the first level of the dungeon. They passed two more guards, but without incident or suspicion, then climbed another set of stairs to the warrior guardhouse, which was attached to the great hall of the castle. Two Shadow Warriors were inside. Their mouths dropped when three prisoners and a Vincero Knight emerged from the dungeon stairwell. One had his sword halfway from its scabbard before he saw Landor.

"What's the meaning of this?" he asked.

Landor produced an evil smile. "Lord Ra has ordered special entertainment at the games tonight."

The warrior relaxed his hand and began to chuckle in a way that brought chills to Duncan.

They exited the guardhouse into the castle yard. Evening had fallen, but once again the castle was illuminated by hundreds of lamps. Music and incense filled the air, for the fete was well underway. This weekly event was far less crowded than the monthly festival, but many youth still danced and frolicked about the castle grounds. The sporting games had begun, and a large crowd had gathered around the arena, cheering loudly.

Landor steered their small procession toward the arena until the guardhouse door closed. Then he motioned with his sword toward the shadows of an awning, and the four knights found temporary cover there. Duncan glanced out at the many guards and knights stationed throughout the castle and began to wonder if there was any hope their plan would succeed. He looked up to the gallery and again saw the ominous figure of Lord Ra standing there, reveling in the power of his fete. Two powerful knights wearing capes stood beside him.

Duncan assumed Kendrick's response to this situation would be calculated and composed...but he was not Kendrick. Although he greatly admired those qualities in his mentor and desired them for himself, he could not stop the flood of anxiety that swept over him as he stared up at the lord of the castle. He concentrated on turning the anxiety into anger over this foolish destruction of lives and Ra's propagation of evil to the lands beyond.

He looked over to Kinley and Gregory. They were brave knights, and if they felt fear they did not show it.

It was Landor's countenance that surprised Duncan the most. He was staring up at Lord Ra from the shadows of their hiding place, frozen by the sight. In the brief time that Duncan had known him, the man had manifested nothing but strength. But here in the domain of his former master, he seemed to quake at the sight of Ra.

Duncan came to him and grasped his shoulder. "We can do this, Landor."

Landor slowly brought his gaze to Duncan. "It has been many years since I've seen the master," Landor whispered. "He is…too powerful!"

"Remember the Prince." Duncan clenched his jaw.

Landor blinked and truly looked into Duncan's eyes. "Yes." Landor nodded and said again, "Yes."

"There is Ancel!" Kinley pointed across the courtyard to the opposite side of the games arena. Elise's brother was staring in their direction.

"We must make our way to the barbican." Landor motioned toward the gatehouse. "There we will find the winches that control the drawbridge and the gates."

The barbican was the tall face of the central gatehouse that proclaimed the castle's magnificence to the outside world. It soared even higher than the seven massive towers of the octagonal-shaped castle wall. Duncan remembered the gatehouse was flanked by two portcullises, or massive gates of iron grating, one facing the drawbridge and one opening to the inner courtyard. Securing only one would mean disaster for the entire mission.

"The gatehouse will be guarded by Ra's Shadow Warriors," Landor warned. "Not even a Vincero Knight is allowed within. Once we reach the doorway, they will immediately become suspicious."

"We must split up and mingle with the crowd," Duncan said. "We are too conspicuous together. I'll make my way to Ancel and tell him to wait until we are nearer the gatehouse."

"Agreed," Landor said. "Duncan, the guards and the regular knights are not of great concern, but you and I must avoid the Shadow Warriors and any Vincero Knights at all cost. We are fortunate those two warriors in the guardhouse didn't recognize us. Thus far I have only seen the two Vinceros standing beside Ra, but that doesn't mean there aren't more. Be watchful!"

"How will I identify them?" Gregory asked.

"Within the castle, all Vinceros wear a cape of their own color."

"Like yours?" Gregory motioned with his chin toward Landor's swirling cape. Landor looked startled, as if he had forgotten what he was wearing. Then he nodded. "Time to go."

Duncan grabbed Kinley's and Gregory's arms. "Smile," he said with a wide grin and brightened eyes.

The three Knights of the Prince moved out to mix with the youth of the fete while Landor began working his way through various halls toward the gatehouse. Duncan smiled and danced his way to the opposite side of the castle grounds, mingling with various groups of four or five other youth and keeping a careful lookout for Vinceros and Shadow Warriors.

He edged along the fence surrounding the games arena, where two youth sparred with cushioned sticks. Duncan made his way to Ancel just as one of the combatants slammed his sparring stick into the chest of his opponent and sent him reeling. The crowd cheered loudly, and Duncan joined them. He cut his cheer short and used the noise to speak to Ancel.

"Wait until you see us near the gatehouse."

Ancel nodded and joined in the cheer. Duncan moved on, hoping to hide himself in a group of young men who stood between the games arena and the dance floor. But after just a few paces he felt a soft and tender arm wrap itself around his.

"Hey there, handsome. How about spending some time with me?" A saucy young woman stepped directly in front of him. She was beautiful, and Duncan was momentarily flustered.

"I…ah…" He looked up and saw Gregory partway to the gatehouse.

"Come on." The lass placed her left hand on his neck and began to dance to the enticing music that filled the air. She moved closer to Duncan and batted long lashes up at him.

Duncan took hold of the girl's arms and tried to gently pull them away, but she clung to him all the more. He tried to smile and step away. "I'm sorry… I can't."

The girl would not be dissuaded. Then, suddenly, she was pushed to the side.

"Back off, wench! This one's with me." Kinley grabbed Duncan's arm as she stepped between him and the other girl. She gave the lass a fierce look as though she was ready for a fight.

"Kinley…there you are!" Duncan threw an arm around his fellow knight's shoulder. The other girl put her hands on her hips, gave a huff, and walked away.

"Come, Algernon…dance with me," Kinley said loudly. She took his hand, pulling him toward the musicians and ultimately toward the gatehouse. Once clear of the crowd in the games arena, Kinley released his hand.

"Algernon?" Duncan said.

Kinley shrugged.

"Thanks," Duncan said. She nodded.

After more careful maneuvering, Duncan, Gregory, and Kinley were as close to the gatehouse as they dared go. Duncan tried to locate Landor but couldn't see him at first. Then Gregory nudged Duncan and motioned with his head.

Duncan followed his gaze upward and saw Landor waiting on a raised walkway that led to a doorway in the side of the gatehouse. All was ready.

Duncan was leaning in to say something to Gregory when something caught his eye. He looked up to see impending disaster—Sir Casimir striding across the courtyard toward the three of them. Duncan's stomach rose to his throat, for they had no weapons to defend themselves. He positioned himself behind Gregory and Kinley, hoping that by some miracle Casimir wouldn't see his face. But his Vincero's gait was so quick and his countenance so fierce that Duncan was quite without hope. He held his breath and waited.

"Step aside!" Casimir commanded, pushing Gregory and Kinley apart.

Remarkably, he had not yet drawn his sword, and Duncan resolved in his mind that he would fight with his hands if need be. Perhaps that would give the others enough distraction to make the guardhouse.

Casimir raised his hand to Duncan's shoulder. "Move, I said!" Casimir pushed him aside, and Duncan realized the man's gaze was fixated on the walkway above. Casimir hadn't even looked at his face.

Duncan allowed himself to be pushed and stepped away with a sigh of relief. Then he gasped, realizing Casimir's destination. The evil knight was heading straight for the staircase that would take him to Landor.

With each step that Casimir took, his scowl deepened. His azure cape whipped back and forth in the fury of his travel. Duncan stood frozen, wondering whether he should shout an alarm to Landor.

Then Landor looked down. Casimir and Landor locked eyes, and with that single glance, the battle of Bel Lione began.

At the base of the staircase, Casimir drew his sword and started up the steps at a full run. Landor waited on the walkway with sword in hand.

"Fire! Fire!" one of the guards atop the castle wall shouted as he pointed to the wood and straw shelters near the games arena. The commotion that ensued was nothing short of pandemonium.

Ancel had done his job well. Everyone's attention was turned to the opposite end of the castle yard, where the blaze quickly grew into a roaring fire…everyone's attention except Casimir's. He continued his rush upon Landor.

"Now!" Duncan cried and ran toward the walkway just beneath Landor.

Landor threw back his cape and reached for the swords of his companions. He threw them off the walkway just as Casimir reached him. Duncan arrived just in time to grab the hilt of his sword out of midair. The other two blades stuck into the grass of the yard and were quickly recovered by Gregory and Kinley.

The sound of Landor's clashing sword mixed with the shouts of the people and the roar of a blazing fire. Guards and knights were calling for water, and many ran toward the far end of the castle yard. Casimir tried to shout an alarm to other knights, but his warnings were lost in the commotion, and he was kept busy by Landor's sword.

Duncan, Gregory, and Kinley burst in through the doorway of one side of the gatehouse. Four Shadow Warriors stood inside a small chamber. The nearest occupant was staring out the window that faced the castle yard. He reached for his sword, but Duncan rushed him before he could position himself. The warrior fell to the ground with a thud.

This gatehouse chamber housed two of the three winches they were looking for. Duncan deduced that these two winches controlled the inner and outer gates and that the drawbridge winch must be in the room above, where Landor was attempting to gain access. One winch sat midway between Duncan and the other Shadow Warriors. But the other was on the far side of the room, behind the warriors, next to a staircase that rose toward an upper chamber.

Two of the other warriors drew their swords and advanced toward Duncan and his friends. A third grabbed a large wooden mallet and struck the release latch on the farthest winch. Duncan cringed as he saw the drum of the winch whir into rotation. He heard the outer gate slide down the recesses in the wall and crash into the ground. The warrior who had released it ran to the staircase at the front of the gatehouse.

"Intruders!" he yelled.

Duncan, Gregory, and Kinley rushed the other two warriors to keep them from recovering the nearest winch. Duncan fought one of the warriors, while Kinley and Gregory engaged the other. The third warrior drew his sword but also kept the mallet, waiting for a chance to lower the inner gate.

Then Duncan gasped. In the room above them, he heard the slow but steady clank of a chain winding upon itself.

The drawbridge was rising, and they couldn't stop it.

Behind them, in the yard, chaos still reigned, but the distraction of the fire at the other end of the castle wouldn't last long. Landor's fight with Casimir was in the open, and Lord Ra would soon send the rest of his forces upon them. With the drawbridge up, Kendrick's forces outside would have no way of entering the castle.

Duncan began to despair, for all seemed lost.

"Charge!" Kendrick shouted.

The glow and smoke of a fire rose up and out of the walls of the castle of Bel Lione, signaling Kendrick's force to attack.

Kendrick galloped forward upon Pilgrim with his sword before him, rushing toward an enemy of two kingdoms. Five hundred horses thundered behind him toward the castle drawbridge. The two large warriors on the near side of the bridge drew their swords and ran across the bridge shouting an alarm.

I hope you have been successful, my friends, Kendrick thought, *or this charge will quickly cease.*

The castle of Bel Lione loomed larger with each stride Pilgrim took. With a third of the distance yet to cover, Kendrick's heart sank. Beyond the castle drawbridge, he saw the outer portcullis slam down and shut off the entrance to the castle.

He hesitated, but Pilgrim did not. He was fully committed, caught up in the momentum of battle. Kendrick kicked the steed to an even faster gallop…just as the edge of the drawbridge began to rise from the near bank of the moat.

By the time Kendrick reached the drawbridge, its edge was already waist high. Pilgrim seemed to know his rider's heart and jumped onto the rising platform. Kendrick heard several more do the same behind him.

Pilgrim nearly lost his footing on the bridge's sloping surface, but he regained his balance and continued his gallop toward the castle. Two Shadow Warriors stood waiting, one on each side of the bridge. Kendrick guided Pilgrim toward the warrior on the right.

The warrior readied his blade for a strike at Kendrick, but Pilgrim slammed him to the ground and trampled him beneath. Kendrick glanced backward to see Winston charging down the other side of the bridge, while three other riders struggled to maintain control of their mounts on the increasing slope of the bridge.

The second warrior plunged his sword into Winston's horse. The animal screamed and stumbled. Winston tumbled to the ground, rolling up against the castle wall. The warrior was upon him instantly, but Kendrick turned Pilgrim about and charged on the warrior just as he was aiming a vertical cut toward Winston. Kendrick's sword sliced through the warrior's torso and stopped the blow before it began.

The five knights were now trapped on the narrow outer yard between the castle wall and the moat. Kendrick looked up, fully expecting to be pummeled with stones and arrows from above at any moment. Across the moat, he could see the rest of his force milling about anxiously.

"What do we do?" one of the knights asked.

Kendrick dismounted, walked over to the gate, and peered through the grating. He was encouraged by the fact that the inner portcullis had not yet fallen closed. That meant someone within was still alive and fighting.

Beyond the gatehouse passageway, the fire still burned in the castle yard. Guards and knights worked to extinguish it, while young men and women wandered in confusion. Some pressed toward the gatehouse. Kendrick shouted for them to stay back.

Suddenly he saw three large figures cross from right to left on the far side of the gateway. Shadow Warriors! Kendrick feared greatly for Duncan, Landor, and the others, for if they were preoccupied with a fight within the gatehouse, these three warriors would surely overtake and kill them.

"Come!" Kendrick called to the men and motioned to the gate. They sheathed their swords and tried to lift the portcullis, but it would not move. They tried once more and then gave up.

"All is lost." One of the knights stared up at the massive gate towers, where heads began to appear, for now the castle was at full alarm. The drawbridge had reached the halfway point and gave no indication of stopping. All seemed lost indeed! 🔲

CHAPTER EIGHTEEN

THE BATTLE OF BEL LIONE

 The clang of swords echoed inside the gatehouse, where Duncan was heavily engaged with a merciless Shadow Warrior. The blows were almost too powerful for him to bear. Gregory and Kinley seemed to be holding their ground, for they had a divergent advantage, but Duncan retreated slowly across the floor, wondering what would happen when he was pinned against the wall.

Above him, in the upper chamber of the gatehouse, the drawbridge chain still clanked, and the sounds of a scuffle filtered down the stairwell. Any minute now, more Shadow Warriors would arrive, and his group's window of opportunity would be closed.

Duncan heard the gatehouse door open behind him and knew the enemy must be at hand. Then the face of the warrior before him went slack with fear and a deep voice boomed from the doorway. "The King reigns!"

"And His Son!" Duncan and his fellow knights responded with a surge of fresh enthusiasm as three huge figures joined the fight. They quickly cut down the Shadow Warriors, then moved to lock the gatehouse door.

"Thank you," Duncan gasped, still breathing heavily. One of the newcomers nodded toward Duncan, and he recognized him as the man who had lifted him from Casimir's window back in Attenbury. The commander of the group was a giant warrior with shining ebony skin and a strong square jaw. Duncan realized he must be the Silent Warrior Kendrick had told him about.

"You are Bronwyn?" he asked.

The big warrior nodded gravely.

"Where did you come from?" Kinley asked.

"The tunnel…behind you," Bronwyn said. "Barden, raise the gate. Everyone else to the upper gatehouse. We must lower the drawbridge, or this assault is over!"

The Silent Warrior named Barden set to the task of winding the chain of the outer gate onto the drum of the winch. His bronzed muscles rippled with each turn. Bronwyn led the rest of them up the gatehouse stairs toward the upper chamber, where the sound of a skirmish was still evident.

When Duncan reached the top stair, he saw Landor in the fight of his life against two Shadow Warriors. The door behind him was shut and bolted from within and someone, presumably Casimir, kept pounding on the far side, trying to break it down. Two other Shadow Warriors were at the winch, working feverishly to raise the drawbridge.

In a moment the small room was filled with flashing swords and the shouts of warring knights and warriors. One of the Shadow Warriors stayed on the drawbridge winch until the last possible moment and then set the release latch of the winch to secure it.

"Kinley!" Duncan pointed to a large mallet in the corner of the room. He engaged the warrior at the winch and tried to force him into retreat, but he stood firm. Duncan stole a glance toward Landor and was relieved to see that one of his adversaries had disengaged to face Bronwyn.

Duncan's foe made a wide powerful slice from his left. Duncan brought his sword up from beneath. Their swords clashed, and he carried the collision of steel up and over his head. Once the blades passed above him, he swept his sword in a circular arc to execute an upward diagonal slice toward the face of the warrior. It found its mark, and the warrior roared in pain, stumbling backward.

Duncan pressed him further, and Kinley leapt to the winch, mallet in hand. Duncan thought she was still too close to the blade of the wounded warrior, but he also knew the blow of her mallet would change the course of this battle.

The warrior recovered from the pain of the gash across his face and advanced on Kinley with a deadly vertical cut just as she swung the mallet toward the release latch. Duncan shouted and moved to cover her, but he wondered if his sword could possibly reach her before the Shadow Warrior's grisly weapon did. It was a moment that would determine the fate of many.

"Kendrick," Winston shouted, "it's moving!"

Kendrick returned his attention to the iron portcullis, and his hope was renewed when he saw the pointed bottom edge of the gate lift out of the ground. The men instinctively tried to help it rise.

Kendrick looked back at the drawbridge, which seemed frozen in its half-raised position. "Come on, Duncan," he muttered, "get that bridge down!"

The gate was now as high as their knees. Kendrick dropped to the ground and rolled beneath it, and the other four knights followed. They ran through the gatehouse passage to meet the front edge of the crowd of panic-stricken youth. Behind them and up on the castle walls, Kendrick saw the guards, knights, and warriors rushing toward the front of the castle.

The push of the crowd had nearly forced Kendrick and his men back into the passage when they heard the wild rattle of chains unrolling.

Kendrick turned to see the drawbridge of the castle falling rapidly until it crashed upon the far bank of the moat. Five hundred mounted knights pounded across the bridge just as the mob of youth came running onto it. A few of these jumped into the moat when they saw the advancing horses, but most ran into the outer yard and away from the chaos of the castle. Screams of hysteria, shouts, clanging swords, and thumping hoofbeats filled the night.

Kendrick wondered at the fate of his friends. They had been successful, but at what cost? Remembering his promise to Lady Odette, he looked for Ancel in the crowd of youths, but it was an impossible search in all of the mayhem.

Kendrick managed to push his way against the crowd of onrushing youths and into the castle yard just as the first of his mounted knights came through the gatehouse. He looked across the castle grounds to the gallery of the great hall, where a dark, looming figure stood issuing commands to men below. The congestion at the gate had bought time for Lord Ra and his forces to recover from the fire and the surprise attack. Now they rallied and began to advance on Kendrick's position.

Kendrick shouted to his closest companions to take up positions beside him. "We must defend the gatehouse until all of our forces are in!"

Within a few moments all of Ra's men were upon them, and the battle raged fiercely. Kendrick looked to the gatehouse to check if it was secure and saw Casimir descending the steps of the walkway to join in the fracas. Two castle guards carrying axes met him on the staircase. They pressed against the railing to allow the Vincero to pass. Instead, he jumped from midway down the stairs onto an unsuspecting mounted Knight of the Prince, dragging the man to the ground. The two men scrambled for a moment, but Casimir was first to find his footing. With one clean thrust, he plunged his sword into the knight's chest.

"Casimir!" Kendrick shouted as his comrade fell.

Casimir jerked his head about, and Kendrick looked once again into those dark eyes of hate. The two men rushed upon each other. Kendrick lifted his sword, feeling the power of the Prince surge through it as never before.

In the throes of such a battle a hundred decisions are made in seconds, and the fate of a life can hinge upon each one. Casimir was first to advance with a combination that Kendrick deflected and finished by parrying a thrust. He quickly countered with a slice and a diagonal cut. Casimir caught the slice with his blade and attempted a quick counter-slice at Kendrick's head, but Kendrick predicted the move, ducked beneath the blade, and brought an arcing slice that tore into Casimir's right shoulder. Casimir yelled and fell back against the support of the walkway.

Kendrick advanced and held his sword to his chest, for Casimir's arm hung limply at his side. "Yield, Casimir," he shouted. "This battle is not against you but against Ra!"

"Never!" Casimir transferred his sword to his left hand and swung it deftly toward Kendrick. Their fight resumed, but soon Kendrick brought a two-handed cut so powerfully to Casimir's sword that it flew from his hand. Casimir drew a long-knife and lunged toward Kendrick, but Kendrick recovered the position of his sword and thrust it into the chest of his oncoming foe. Casimir's eyes continued to spew hatred as he fell.

The two men with axes stood on the upper walkway now, chopping at the gatehouse door. Kendrick reached the bottom of the stairs just as they broke through, only to be met by a masterful and deadly sword. Within seconds one lay prone on the walkway, the other had fallen over the edge of the railing, and their white-haired assailant was turning back into the gatehouse.

"Landor!" Kendrick shouted up to his friend and could not help the brief smile that crossed his lips even in the midst of such a fierce battle. The two of them met on the stairway.

"Duncan?" Kendrick asked.

"He's fine." Landor nodded toward the gatehouse. "He's caring for Kinley."

Kendrick gave Landor a look of concern.

"Her arm is cut badly, but she'll be all right," Landor said. "She risked her life to get that bridge down."

"It made all the difference. I think most of our knights are in the castle now, and it looks like most of the young people have—"

"Kendrick, look." Landor had grabbed Kendrick's arm and now pointed across the castle yard toward the warrior guardhouse and the great hall. Another one hundred fifty Shadow Warriors were emerging to join the fight.

"There are too many," the older man muttered. "It's impossible."

"Nothing's impossible." Kendrick started down the steps. "Come, Landor. The Prince is with us!"

Landor followed. But before they reached the bottom of the staircase, they heard the shout of one voice rise above the sounds of the battle.

"Ramsey!" Bronwyn shouted from the walkway above them. His deep voice echoed off the massive walls. He held his magnificent sword before him, pointing across the expanse of the castle grounds.

The battle seemed to pause as these two warriors of old faced each other, no longer as friends, but as irreconcilable enemies. Ra left the gallery and shortly appeared at the door of the great hall. Kendrick and Landor separated and threw themselves into the fight in the castle yard as Bronwyn ran toward the duel that awaited him at center stage of the castle.

The Knights of the Prince battled bravely, but they were clearly outnumbered, and fresh reinforcements were still emerging from the dungeon. Kendrick sensed the tide was turning against them. He wondered how long his comrades could hold out.

Suddenly the sound of many horses' hooves came pounding like a storm charging across the plains.

"Kendrick!" Winston shouted in despair at the ominous sight of the unknown warriors pouring through the gates.

"Make way, Winston," Kendrick shouted back as a smile spread across his face. "They are the King's!"

The ranks of the knights parted, and Bronwyn's promised force of more than four hundred Silent Warriors charged straight through to engage the Shadow Warriors. The castle yard soon rang with the clash of swords from two diametrically opposed forces. Both were fighting for the souls of men and women—one to imprison them and one to free them. Bronwyn and Ra engaged in the middle of it all, and the sound of their swords seemed to resound above the rest.

To Kendrick, the battle seemed to rage on forever. In the torchlight, he saw Ra disengage from Bronwyn and put two of his warriors against him instead. He didn't understand why until he saw Ra making his way toward another. Kendrick desperately fought toward Landor, but Ra reached him first.

The fury of Ra's blows upon his former Vincero Knight was unlike anything Kendrick had ever seen, and Landor could only defend and retreat. His face was a mask of fear before the wrath of his former master.

Kendrick was nearly to Landor when a Shadow Warrior engaged him and prevented him from coming to the aid of his friend.

"You brought this to my castle!" he heard Ra say to Landor as he blasted blow after blow onto his sword. "No one betrays Lord Ra and lives—no one!" He made one more vicious cut that tore Landor's sword from his grip and left him helpless.

"*No!*" Kendrick screamed against the inevitable.

Landor looked past Ra to Kendrick, but there was nothing Kendrick could do to stop Ra's blade. It penetrated deep into Landor's abdomen. Kendrick felt as though it pierced his own heart, and an unstoppable fury rose up in him. In two lightning cuts he fell the Shadow Warrior that was keeping him from the lord of the castle.

Ra turned to engage Kendrick. "I find it difficult to believe that one such as you could bring such a battle to my castle," he sneered.

Kendrick did not honor him with a spoken response. He just

launched a volley of furious blows, forcing a surprised Ra into retreat. Twice, Kendrick nearly landed a cut on the Shadow Warrior. Ra recovered with a vertical slice that Kendrick only partially thwarted, his shoulder armor deflecting the sword away from his head.

Kendrick made an arcing cut across Ra's body that he expected Ra to block. Ra stepped back instead, and the momentum of Kendrick's sword carried him too far to the left to counter another vertical cut from Ra. Kendrick continued his turn until his back was to the Shadow Warrior and dropped to one knee. Knowing that Ra's cut from above would be too powerful to stop, Kendrick grabbed the flat of his sword with his gauntleted left hand midway down the blade and held it directly above his head as one would a sparring stick. Ra's blade crashed upon him, but Kendrick's double-handed protection held firm.

With one hand on his hilt and the other still grasping the flat of his blade, Kendrick immediately spun about on his knee and thrust with all of his might into the chest of Ra. The sword pierced the Shadow Warrior's armor. Ra's own sword fell to the ground. His eyes bulged out, and he glared at Kendrick, his face only inches away.

"Impossible!" he gasped.

"You forget," Kendrick said, "I serve the Prince who makes all things possible—even the destruction of evil strongholds!" Kendrick withdrew his sword. Ra collapsed to the ground and gasped his last breath.

A strange hush fell upon the castle. All fighting stopped, and all eyes turned upon Kendrick. He looked up at the faces of the combatants and knew the battle belonged to the Prince.

"It is over—Ra is dead!" Kendrick shouted. "Lay down your weapons."

All around him, Kendrick heard the clink of swords slowly being dropped. Then he heard Landor cough. He ran to his fallen friend and knelt beside him.

"Landor." Kendrick gently lifted Landor's head.

Landor coughed again, and blood began to trickle from the corner of his mouth. Pain wrenched Kendrick's heart, for he knew there was little he could do to stop the inevitable.

"Bronwyn!" Kendrick shouted, hoping against hope that the Silent Warrior could help. Bronwyn came and knelt opposite him, then shook his head slowly.

Landor grabbed Kendrick's surcoat and pulled Kendrick close to him.

"I must…tell you something…" He coughed once more and winced at the pain it brought him.

"Be still, my friend," Kendrick urged.

"No…listen to me." Landor inhaled with great effort. "I need one thing from you before I…" Landor closed his eyes and could not finish the sentence.

Kendrick supported him with his left arm. "Anything, Landor, to my very life." His vision blurred with unfallen tears.

"I…need you to forgive me…" Landor coughed again. "Or kill me now."

Kendrick stared down in confusion, wondering if the pain had addled his friend's thinking. "Landor, there is no offense to forgive," he said. "You have twice saved my life and brought victory to this great battle. I owe you a great debt."

"You don't…understand." Landor fought for another breath. He shook his head from side to side as if to refuse Kendrick's words. "It was…it was I…who killed your wife and young son."

Kendrick froze as his world slowly crumbled around him, the broken pieces of his life rearranging themselves into an image he never expected.

Landor tightened his desperate grip on Kendrick again and pulled himself up to Kendrick with extreme effort. "I led the raid that day… I ordered my men to kill everyone and take your riches. But when I saw the…bodies…their blood upon the stone floor, I…"

Kendrick turned his head away from Landor and clenched his jaw tightly. He wanted to cover his ears and pull away as his own memories of that day pounded down upon him again, but Landor would not let him go.

"Lord Ra made me into a monster. All of the years of evil my hands brought to so many had eaten my soul to…nothingness. But on that day, I could no longer bear…the evil I had wrought."

More blood flowed from his lips, and he choked on it as he struggled for another breath. Then he seemed to rally a little as he told about that day.

"I fell to my knees and wept beside them, knowing my soul would be condemned forever. I ran from Lord Ra and went to die in the desolate places of Arrethtrae. When you first came to me that day in the mountains, I thought the demons of my past had come to haunt me. Instead you brought the story of the Prince and of His forgiveness and great compassion. The truth of such a great love echoed in the well of sorrow I had dug for myself, and…I had to know more. In spite of my pain…your pain."

Landor paused, fighting for breath, his eyes glittering in the torchlight. "I would die a million deaths to bring back your wife and son. I thought perhaps if I could save your life or give my life for you that it would go away…but it remains…"

He fell back, gasping, and reached for Kendrick's hand, clenching it with white knuckles. "That is why I ask you to forgive me…that I might die in peace. Or else pierce me through with your sword that I might die with your pain."

Kendrick felt as though his own blood had emptied from his veins, and the weight of his own body seemed multiplied a hundredfold. He didn't know how to respond or even what to believe.

Landor's grip on Kendrick's arm began to loosen as the strength drained from him. He convulsed in pain, and his breathing became short and interrupted.

Kendrick sat still, not daring to move. The vengeance he had craved in the past fought to rise within him, but the words of the Prince would not be moved from his mind or his heart. He stood in the fray of a warring heart. One side screamed for revenge…the other whispered mercy.

Landor grabbed Kendrick's hand, which was still wrapped around the hilt of his sword. "Quickly, Kendrick. There is time to execute your vengeance before death steals it from you! I welcome the sting of death, for perhaps it will end the pain of my soul."

Kendrick turned back to look upon Landor, and his inner war ceased. He lifted his sword and laid the hilt upon Landor's chest.

"My sword belongs to the Prince—not to Lucius." Kendrick released his grip on the sword and lifted Landor partly off the bloodstained ground beneath. "Be at peace, my friend," he said softly. "I forgive you!"

Landor's eyes once again filled with tears, and his countenance became peaceful. With the last of his strength he reached up and touched Kendrick's cheek. "If…" Landor coughed and strained for his words. "If I could live again and have a son, I would wish him to be you."

Landor's hand fell to the ground. His eyes closed, and Kendrick felt his body relax.

"Landor!" Kendrick lowered himself close to his friend.

Landor opened his eyes partway. "The pain is gone, my son…for I believe."

His final breath came, and Kendrick gently lowered his body to the ground. He stayed beside his friend for a moment until he felt the steady hand of Duncan on his shoulder.

"He rescued us each," Duncan said quietly. "And now you have rescued him."

Kendrick stood and beheld a scene of victory and surrender.

The battle of Bel Lione was over. ▨

CHAPTER NINETEEN

SET THE CAPTIVES FREE!

 Some of the Silent Warriors set immediately to treating the wounds of Kendrick's knights while Bronwyn and the rest of his men bound the Shadow Warriors and prepared to depart.

"Where will you take them?" Kendrick asked Bronwyn.

"There is a place prepared for them where they will not be able to influence Arrethtraens anymore…at least not for a long while."

The two men looked at each other for a moment.

"Thank you, Bronwyn," Kendrick finally said.

The Silent Warrior's lips slowly curved into a broad smile. Kendrick was stunned. He hadn't thought this stern commander was capable of such a jovial expression.

"No, Sir Kendrick, thank *you*!" Bronwyn nodded and turned to leave.

He and his companions walked through the castle gates and disappeared once more into the realm of secrecy.

Winston and Duncan appeared at Kendrick's side. "The castle is secure. Three hundred twenty-three of Ra's knights and guards and some other castle workers are under guard in the games arena. Sir Casimir is dead, but the other two Vincero Knights are being held separately as you asked."

Kendrick nodded. Uncertain about how to handle the Vincero Knights, he had determined they would be taken to Chessington for the council to decide their fate.

"What now, sir?" Winston and Duncan waited for the next command.

Kendrick's eyes narrowed, and he turned his head toward the warrior guardhouse in the shadows at the back of the castle yard. "Now I fulfill my promise. Come!"

Kendrick walked over to the assembly of guards and ordinary knights in the games arena. They had all been disarmed and forced to sit on the ground, guarded by eighty Knights of the Prince.

Kendrick slowly paced back and forth in front of them, looking down into the eyes of men and women who had served Ra faithfully. Some defied his gaze, and others turned away. It was obvious they all feared him, for he had defeated the mighty Lord Ra in a sword fight.

Kendrick drew his sword, and every captive man and woman there turned their eyes to him.

"We do not take prisoners!" he shouted.

Now even his own knights stood in silence. Duncan and Winston looked at Kendrick with great concern on their faces. A few of the captives cringed.

Kendrick thought of the men and women who had been tormented, imprisoned, and killed in this dreadful place, and his countenance showed his great anger. He pointed to the Shadow Warriors' guardhouse with his sword. "Who among you have entered that guardhouse?" he demanded.

Silence was his only reply until one knight finally spoke.

"It is not allowed," he said.

"Then who among you knows what lies beneath this great castle of pleasures and indulgences?" He gazed from face to face, looking for someone to answer, but no one did...or dared.

He pointed his sword at the knight who had spoken last. "You. What lies beneath?"

The knight looked at his fellow captives for a response of some sort and then looked back to Kendrick. "It is said to be an abandoned dungeon from the foundation of an older castle."

Kendrick stepped over other captives to reach the speaker. He held his sword as if to strike the man down. "Is that what you believe?"

The knight winced. "I don't know what to believe," he said quietly.

"Is that what you all believe?" Kendrick shouted to all of the captives. Fury was in his heart and in his tone. He walked back to the front of the captives.

"Let me tell you the truth of Ra's castle." He pointed once again to the Shadow Warriors' guardhouse. "Beneath that guardhouse is an entrance to a dungeon that holds hundreds, perhaps thousands, of your fellow countrymen. You have not been protecting the freedom of the region's youth. You have been protecting Ra and his plots to imprison and destroy them!"

There was a stir among the captives. Some looked shocked, some appeared rooted in disbelief.

Kendrick grasped his sword by the blade near the hilt and turned it to show the captives the insignia of the King. "We do not take prisoners," he repeated. "We set them free! We are going into the dungeon to release Ra's prisoners. We have taken your weapons from you, and you are free to leave. But countless men and women will soon be coming up from Ra's dungeons. They will need food, water, and care. If Ra has not blackened your heart completely, then I implore you to stay and help us reverse this horrid legacy by ministering to his victims."

Kendrick sheathed his sword and stood quietly before the sea of stunned faces.

"The choice is yours," Kendrick finally said and motioned for his men to dismiss the group. "Winston, take those who choose to stay along with sixty of our knights to the storehouse. Prepare food, water, and any other supplies you think we might need. Set up a second infirmary in the great hall." He looked to the massive walls and towers of the castle once again. "This castle will now be a place of healing."

"Yes sir," Winston replied and set out to do his duty.

"Duncan, put thirty knights to guard the castle, and bring the rest that are able to the guardhouse. I'll meet you there in just a moment."

Duncan saluted and began giving orders.

Kendrick crossed the yard to the guardhouse and descended the stairwell to the dungeon. On the first level he found a small room that held the keys to the cells. He descended to the second level and navigated his way back through the labyrinth of tunnels lined with cells toward the secret passageway. The sound of his boots echoing through the hall was interrupted only by the moans of the prisoners.

One man reached for him through his cell bars. "I have seen you before...you are not one of them! What is happening? Where are the guards?"

Kendrick paused, hearing the hesitant plea of hope in his voice. "Be patient, sir," he told him gently. "We have come to set you free."

The man's arm slowly fell. "Truly?"

"Truly! But there are so many. You must be patient."

The man sank to the floor and clung to the bars despondently, as if unable to believe. Kendrick proceeded down the corridor, but by the time he reached the next turn, the man was laughing and crying and shouting behind him. "Thank you, good sir...thank you!"

Kendrick continued until he came to the cell whose occupant's face and voice had not left his mind since he met her. At first the cell looked empty, and his heart sank. Had she survived six years in this torment only to die just before he came to free her?

Please—no, he pleaded.

"Teara?" he called, but there was no reply. The shadows were black near the back of the cell. He sorted through the keys until he found one that fit. The clank of its opening echoed off the stone walls, and the hinges creaked so loudly that Kendrick wondered if the door had ever been opened.

Kendrick walked to the dark corner of the cell and knelt down. He put his hand to the floor and felt the form of a frail bony body. He could not tell if she was yet alive. Her back was to him.

"Teara!" he whispered, and put his arms beneath her. He carefully rolled her into his arms and carried her to the front of the cell where he could see her face.

Very slowly, her eyelids lifted—and then opened wide.

"You…you…came back for me."

Kendrick smiled, and his own eyes welled up. "Yes, Teara. I came back for you."

She put her thin arms around his neck, leaned into his chest, and began to sob. Kendrick carried her out of the cell and began his walk back to the stairwell. Other prisoners reached out, and their pleas for help multiplied with each cell he passed.

"We're coming back for you…all of you!" he shouted as he held Teara close.

Kendrick carried Teara up to the guardhouse and into the castle yard. Everyone in the castle became silent as the reality of their purpose as Knights of the Prince materialized in that moment. The cheers started high on the walls and soon filled the whole castle. Teara looked up in wonder at the other knights and then to Kendrick.

"You have saved me." She looked at him as though he were a grand hero.

"Not I, Teara. The Prince has saved you, just as He saved me from my prison."

She smiled and leaned back into his chest. Kendrick turned to his young protégé.

"Sir Duncan, set them all free!"

Duncan's familiar grin spread wide. "Yes sir!"

Word of the battle had spread quickly to the citizens of Bel Lione and the surrounding region. When the sounds of clashing swords and dying men ended, they came; they all came. Soon thousands of people lined the road, drawbridge, and courtyards of the castle, holding up lamps and torches in the winter darkness.

At first the people seemed merely curious or confused. But once the tear-filled reunions between siblings, parents, and friends began, the frenzied search for loved ones also began. Many of the knights became occupied with keeping order both inside and outside the castle. And though joy often prevailed, deep sorrow pierced the heart of many, for not all who had lost a son, daughter, brother, or sister were rewarded. Some had not survived.

Kendrick was standing in the middle of the castle yard, overcome by the sheer responsibility of it all, when an excited, urgent—and familiar— voice came to him.

"Sir Kendrick! Sir Kendrick!" He turned to see Frayne making his way toward him through the crowd. He finally reached Kendrick and grabbed his forearm.

"I was right?" he asked with hope in his eyes.

Kendrick placed a hand on top of Frayne's. "Yes, my friend. You were right."

"My son?" Frayne pleaded.

"I don't know, Frayne. They are still coming out. There are so many."

Frayne hardly knew what to do. "Where do I look?" he asked in a trembling voice. Kendrick's heart broke for him.

"Come with me. I will help you." Kendrick turned him toward the guardhouse.

"Father!" a weak shout came from their right.

Frayne turned to look. "Hamlin!"

A shivering young man limped over to him, and Frayne wept as he embraced him. After a time he stepped back and put his hands to his son's head as if to convince himself he was not an apparition, then hugged him tightly again.

"My son…my son!" Frayne cried over and over.

Kendrick's heart was comforted. He left Frayne to be with his son and walked toward the great hall to look over the impromptu infirmary. Duncan fell in step beside him, looking tired but pleased. "A marvelous thing was done here today," he said.

"Yes." Kendrick draped an arm over Duncan's shoulder. "You did well, young knight—very well."

Duncan looked to the ground and smiled even bigger.

A commotion sounded behind them, and Frayne's voice came through the crowd again.

"There he is!" The tailor was shouting and pointing to Kendrick. "There is the one who has set them free!"

Many of the citizens began to cheer.

"No, Frayne." Kendrick shook his head, but Frayne walked over to him, still clutching the arm of his son.

"Speak to them, Sir Kendrick. They want to know what happened." Frayne insisted. Many nearby shouted in agreement.

Kendrick held up his hands and shook his head, but Duncan put his hand on his shoulder.

"Speak to them, Kendrick," Duncan said.

"I am just a knight, not an orator," Kendrick said.

"You forget, my friend, that the Prince has called us not only to battle but to be heralds above all!"

Kendrick returned Duncan's smile. "The pupil teaches the teacher. I am proud of you, Duncan!"

Duncan led Kendrick to the gatehouse tower so that all within and without the castle could see and hear him. Kendrick looked out over the many thousands of people and felt their need. His heart swelled with compassion, and he began to speak.

"Within the walls of this castle," he told them, his voice ringing clear in the chilly air, "your sons and daughters were taught to live in rebellion to you, to the King, and to His good ways. Such rebellion never brings freedom. It always brings bondage and ultimately death. But there is One who brings true freedom and life. Let me tell you about the Prince…"

CHAPTER TWENTY

PARTING SORROWS

Many weeks passed, and the labor of restoration and healing in Bel Lione seemed endless. The town and her citizens were changing, and Kendrick and Duncan did their best to guide them through it. Their testimony led many to believe in the Prince. They even started a haven where men and women could train to become Knights of the Prince.

Many citizens opened their homes to prior captives who had nowhere to go or were too weak to travel. Lady Odette graciously took in four who needed daily care to strengthen them. Teara was among them, for six years of near starvation had left her in a state that would require months of recovery.

Kendrick, who was also staying at Lionsgate, enjoyed watching Teara slowly blossom into a lovely young woman. Her gentle but confident spirit delighted him, though her presence made him slightly nervous as well. He enjoyed her company more than he had expected, and he wondered how a call to a new mission would affect her…and him.

That time came as winter turned to spring. There were many farewells to make, some much harder than others.

"Sir Kendrick?" Teara stood with Lady Odette's family in the court-yard of Lionsgate as Kendrick and Duncan prepared to leave. "When I am strong again, will you train me to be a knight? I want to serve the Prince as you do."

Kendrick smiled down at the former captive who had grown to be his friend. "Yes, Teara. I will."

Teara took a step toward him and gazed up into his eyes. "Promise?"

Kendrick hesitated, for he knew what that meant. Teara raised an eyebrow, and he found it impossible to refuse her.

He smiled. "I promise."

Teara smiled back, though her eyes were solemn. "I believe you, my good knight, and I thank you once more for saving me."

Kendrick took her hand and brought it to his lips. "I made a promise to you," he said. He released her hand, swung into Pilgrim's saddle, and gazed back down at her. "I always keep my promises."

"Then I shall hold you to it." She stepped back again, eyes glistening. "I wish you a safe journey."

Kendrick nodded and turned to Ancel. "Ancel, your courage honors your father," he said and saluted him. "Thank you for your great help."

Ancel smiled and saluted back. "We shall miss you, sir."

"And I you. Shall we, Duncan?"

Duncan and Elise had been standing a little apart, their heads close together, whispering quietly. Duncan turned to mount his horse, but Elise reached for his arm. "Must you go?"

Duncan turned and placed a gentle hand upon her cheek. "You know that I must. My work for the Prince is far from over, and I have much yet to learn from Sir Kendrick."

Kendrick was somewhat surprised by the comment. He glanced toward Duncan and briefly locked eyes with him. The young man's eyes expressed a fresh respect and admiration for him as a mentor. Kendrick responded with a nearly imperceptible smile, for now the respect was mutual.

Duncan returned his gaze to Elise's sad face. Kendrick could see her soft and gentle ways tugging on Duncan's heart. He was once again amazed at the power a lady could hold over even the mightiest warriors, and he wondered if his future journeys might be made alone.

"I will come back for you, my love." Duncan reached down to take her hand. "Will you wait for me?"

"I will wait for you and you alone, my knight. And though my heart will ache for your return, my love for you will only grow in your absence." Elise lifted herself onto tiptoe and gently kissed Duncan's cheek. She backed away into her mother's embrace and watched Duncan rise onto his mount. A single tear escaped and traced its way down her cheek.

Kendrick patted Pilgrim's neck and then tipped his head to Lady Odette.

"I thank you for your gift, my lady," Kendrick said. "He's a gallant horse."

Lady Odette smiled. "He deserves a worthy knight. Take good care of him…and bring him back to visit soon. You know the way."

Kendrick gave a final wave, reined Pilgrim around, then led Duncan down the tree-lined avenue and through the town of Bel Lione. As the town receded behind them, Kendrick turned toward Duncan. He could tell his young companion's mind was still back with Elise, cherishing the memory of their departure and her farewell kiss.

"Duncan," Kendrick said.

"Yes?" Duncan jerked back to the present.

"There's a kingdom out there that needs the hope of the Prince and freedom from the chains of the Dark Knight. But…she is a lady worth returning for."

Duncan smiled broadly and then set his eyes on the horizon.

"Then what are we waiting for?" he replied, and kicked his horse into a spirited run.

"Ah, the zest of a youthful heart," Kendrick said with a smile. "And for you, my Prince, I pray that my heart will never be found old or lazy!"

Kendrick urged Pilgrim to a matching gallop and joined his young friend on a journey deeper into the heart of the King's land, fulfilling their call to be noble Knights of Arrethtrae.

THE WINDS
OF ARRETHTRAE

The story of Sir Kendrick and Sir Duncan does indeed compel me to commit their adventures to parchment, lest the testimony of their mighty deeds be forgotten. Their stand was strong and their courage sure, for the power of the Prince inflamed their hearts.

The destruction of Lord Ra's stronghold at Bel Lione was no small advancement for the kingdom of the Prince, for it struck a two-edged sword deep into the very heart of Lucius's realm. Take heart and hear the call of the Prince as did Sir Kendrick and Sir Duncan, for I am certain that your region of the kingdom needs young men and women of great courage to rise up, proclaim the Prince, and fight against the evil one as well.

It is time now to follow the winds of Arrethtrae away from these two noble knights and seek for others.

Perhaps the winds of the kingdom will linger near you!

DISCUSSION QUESTIONS

Review Questions from the Kingdom Series

Much of the allegorical symbolism in the Knights of Arrethtrae originated in the Kingdom Series. Here are a few questions to review this symbolism:

1. Who does the Prince represent?
2. Who are the Knights of the Prince?
3. Who are the Noble Knights?
4. What is Chessington? Arrethtrae?
5. Who is the Dark Knight/Lucius?
6. Who are the Silent Warriors and the Shadow Warriors?
7. What is a haven?

Questions for *Sir Kendrick and the Castle of Bel Lione*

CHAPTER 1

1. Kendrick tells Augustus that the ways of the Prince always seem contrary to the rest of the kingdom. What does he mean? Read Ephesians 2:8–9.
2. Find a Bible verse that supports Kendrick's statement during his discussion with Duncan that their purpose should be to make a name for the Prince, not for themselves. Can you think of a skill or strength that you possess that could be used to bring glory to the Lord instead of to yourself? How might you use it?
3. The prestige of the Knights of the Prince resides in their cause and not in their dwellings. Think of a few ways to restate this to fit your own life, your family's life, and the church Jesus established through His disciples.
4. What does the Council of Knights represent?

5. Read Ephesians 6:12. When William says, "Our battle is always with the Dark Knight.... Be sure that some other order or guild will rise up to unwittingly do the bidding of this evil warrior," to what is he referring? Discuss some instances of this in your own experience.

6. In chapter 1 we learn of the sad outcome for the family who housed the two Knights of the Prince. Read 2 Timothy 3:10–12; 1 Peter 4:12–16; and Acts 5:41. What do these verses say about persecution? Do you know of any specific examples of Christians experiencing persecution for their faith in the world today?

7. William advises that it is unwise to dwell on the plots of Lucius instead of focusing on their mission for the Prince. Although we shouldn't dwell on the plots of the devil, 2 Corinthians 2:11 says that we are not to be ignorant of Satan's devices. How can being aware of these devices help us live more victorious Christian lives? What might happen if a Christian moves from being aware of the devices of the devil to being preoccupied with the plots of the devil?

Chapter 2

1. Duncan teases Kendrick because he is ignorant of Kendrick's past and the pain that lingers there. Have you had a similar misunderstanding in which you learned that it is important and wise to choose words very carefully? If so, what was it?

2. Why do you think Kendrick only wanted to participate in the Skill at Arms event? Why do you think he decides to participate in all of the events after telling Duncan he would only participate in the Skill at Arms? How does this apply to us as believers?

3. Kendrick tells Duncan he wishes he could erase his tournament experiences from his past. Can you find a Bible verse that might comfort him, now that he is a Knight of the Prince?

CHAPTER 3

1. Kendrick tells Duncan of Casimir, "When a man's eye is so full of evil that no good remains within, then evil will do what evil does regardless of the presence of good without." Matthew 6:22–23 says, "The light of the body is the eye: if therefore thine eye be single, thy whole body shall be full of light. But if thine eye be evil, thy whole body shall be full of darkness. If therefore the light that is in thee be darkness, how great is that darkness!" (KJV). These verses contrast darkness with light. With what do they contrast evil? What do you think this means?

2. Kendrick says that being friendly to Casimir is like heaping coals of fire on his head. Find a Bible passage that supports this statement. Is it easy to accept the concept behind this verse? Why or why not?

CHAPTER 4

1. Duncan feels the need to prove himself as a knight. To whom does he want to prove himself? Is this a proper aspiration?

2. What kind of emotion usually accompanies the glare that the giant man gives Duncan? Why do you think he responds this way?

CHAPTER 5

1. Each book of the Knights of Arrethtrae Series deals with a specific set of vices and virtues. One of these vices—impulsiveness—is demonstrated by Duncan, who foolishly took action alone and without counsel. Find some Bible verses that support Kendrick's reason for his anger with Duncan.

2. Would it be as easy for you as it is for Kendrick to give up the chance to be the champion? Explain in your own words his motivation for withdrawing.

CHAPTER 6

1. Another vice that *Sir Kendrick and the Castle of Bel Lione* deals with is alluded to in this chapter and is hidden in the names of the lord of the castle and the city in which the castle is located. What word is formed by the sounds of the combination of these three words? A vice can easily become a stronghold in a person's life or in a community. In what ways is this vice (or stronghold) demonstrated among the citizens of Bel Lione?

2. Considering the above information, what do you think the festival might represent? Why do you think no one attends the festival just once? Why do you think the festival participants are different when they return?

CHAPTER 7

1. As Duncan becomes more stable and focused on his mission for the Prince, his partnership with Kendrick improves greatly. What are some of the effects of being focused on the Lord?

CHAPTER 8

1. Although Duncan's intentions were good, it was foolish for him to enter the castle. List two reasons why it was foolish. How does this apply to Christians?

2. Can you think of a time when you experienced the "powerful pull" of temptation as Duncan does at the festival? How did you respond to it? What do you think are some wise and effective methods of dealing with temptation?

3. Duncan realizes that in spite of their appearance of strength and power, the Shadow Warriors fear the power of the Prince. Why is this so? Find some verses that show this.

CHAPTER 9

1. Kendrick proclaims to the two Shadow Warriors, "Though my blood may spill, I am not afraid of you." What resource does he draw on that gives him this courage? What does this represent biblically?

2. Find the passages in the Bible that tell about the rebellion of Lucifer and his angels.

3. Can you describe why you think Bronwyn is so upset and angry? Have you ever watched something evil gain power and strength and greatly wanted to stop it? What did you do?

CHAPTER 10

1. Morley says, "I can see in your face that you have lost one to Lord Ra...like so many before you. Others have come to me, but I can offer them nothing except this: the choice was their own, and their own shall they bear.... Mourn not for the foolish, though they be your sons or daughters, for darkness swallows all who play in its shadows." Give some examples of how people choose to "play in the shadows" of darkness.

2. Ancel says, "I didn't want to become like them—truly, Mother. I just wanted to see what the festival was like." Why is this a dangerous attitude?

3. What are some ways that the stronghold of rebellion is manifested in the youth once they enter the castle at the festival?

CHAPTER 11

1. While Kendrick's words could not convey that he had come in peace, he found a way to convince Landor. How did he do it? What did he display that encouraged Landor to consider his requests? What does this say about the way we live as Christians?

CHAPTER 12

1. Kendrick says, "Let me tell you of the bread that brings hope and life to all who eat of it." What is he talking about? Find a Bible verse or passage that speaks of this bread.

2. Have you seen the story of Jesus transform a life such as how the Prince's story changed Kendrick? How does observing that change make you feel? What does it do for your own faith?

3. The names of the blood wolves that protect Lord Ra's castle are Hypoc, Deceptor, Toxica, Revel, Plezior, Arrogoy, Destroyer, Carnage, Chaos, and Tormentor. What do you think these beasts represent?

4. Kendrick is resolved to save Duncan, even after having to travel high into the mountains to find the mysterious Landor and then hearing him speak of all the dangerous obstacles he would have to meet in order to find Duncan, who Landor believes is already dead. Though the situation seems all but hopeless, Kendrick remains steadfast in his mission to rescue his friend. Loyalty is one of the virtues focused on in *Sir Kendrick and the Castle of Bel Lione*. What kinds of obstacles did Jesus face in order to be loyal to the Father and to us in His mission to rescue mankind?

CHAPTER 13

1. As Kendrick moves closer to the castle and Ra's forces, he begins to experience fear. Find a verse about overcoming fear. If we are believers in Jesus Christ, why don't we have to be afraid? (Refer to 1 John 4:4.)

2. Kendrick is hindered in his mission to rescue Duncan by Ra's beasts. First Thessalonians 2:18 says that Paul was also hindered by Satan. In what ways does Satan try to hinder our work for the Lord?

CHAPTER 14

1. Looking into Teara's eyes, Kendrick vows "never to forget her image" because it is "a picture of Lord Ra's work in the souls of men and women." Do you react this way to lost people you encounter? What does Jesus say in Matthew 9:37–38 about reaching the lost?

CHAPTER 15

1. In this chapter, Landor explains the three responses to participating in Ra's festivals. Take some time to consider the three roads a person can take once he decides to enter the stronghold of rebellion.

   A. What is the most common response? When these people grow up, what do they expect from their own children? Why don't they realize what is really going on? What does this response look like in our society? Do you see examples of this response in anyone you know…or even in yourself?

   B. What is the second response? What eventually happens to these people? What kinds of "snares of death" does the devil set for people in our society who respond this way? What are the possible outcomes for people who fall into these traps? Do you know any examples of this response?

   C. What is the response that Lord Ra is most earnestly seeking? What does he do with these people? What are some examples of who these people might be in our society today?

2. There is actually a fourth possible response to Lord Ra's festivals. What is it? How do youth in our society make this response? Can you think of at least one character in the book who chose this response?

3. Near the end of the chapter, Kendrick tells Landor that the Prince came "to restore this land, these people…and to restore you, no matter what you've done." Find two verses that offer salvation to anyone who believes.

CHAPTER 16

1. Kendrick says, "I can promise you one thing. When you say yes to the Prince, you had better hang on tight, for His stallion rides far and fast!" What does Isaiah 64:4 say about God's amazing plans for you? Have you experienced adventure in Christ?

2. Kendrick calls many Knights of the Prince into battle against Lord Ra. What does this symbolize for believers? How do we battle against evil?

3. There are several examples in the Bible of battles in which God used a highly outnumbered force to bring victory to His people. Find one of these instances. Why do you think God did this? Does He still work on this principle today? Have you seen an example of this in your own life (maybe not with numbers, but perhaps with ability or experience)? If yes, what was it?

4. Reread Kendrick's speech to prepare his knights for battle. His powerful words are based on several Bible verses. Can you find the references?

CHAPTER 17

1. As Landor, Duncan, and the other knights neared the castle's dungeon, Duncan started to become fearful and anxious because of his past experiences. How did he deal with this? Look up Matthew 16:24–25. How do these verses apply to us?

CHAPTER 18

1. When Kendrick defeats Ra, he tells Ra that the Prince makes all things possible. Find a Bible verse that supports this. Have you seen an example of this in your own life or the life of someone close to you?

2. Kendrick and the other Knights of the Prince are victorious over the stronghold of rebellion. Find a Bible verse that assures us of having power through God to destroy strongholds.

3. When Landor reveals the truth of his past to Kendrick, Kendrick struggles between the way of his former life and his new life in the Prince. What is it that finally draws Kendrick to forgive Landor? What does this symbolize for Christians? Forgiveness is another virtue addressed in *Sir Kendrick and the Castle of Bel Lione.* Why is forgiveness so important? What does Colossians 2:13–15 say about forgiveness?

4. What is it that finally convinces Landor to believe in the Prince, and how is this an example for Christians?

CHAPTER 19

1. Bronwyn tells Kendrick he is taking the Shadow Warriors to a "place prepared for them where they will not be able to influence Arrethtraens anymore…at least not for a long while." What does he mean?

2. When Kendrick brings Teara up out of the dungeon, he refuses the credit for setting her free. Instead, he tells her that the Prince saved her, just as He saved Kendrick from his own prison. What was that prison? What other kinds of "prisons" does Jesus set people free from?

3. The reunion scene at the end of chapter 19 is a picture of the joy and healing that the Lord can bring when He frees a lost child from rebellion and brings him home, repentant,

to his family. Can you find a similar story in one of Jesus'
parables?

4. When Kendrick is preparing to share the story of the Prince
   with the citizens of Bel Lione, he looks out over the many
   thousands of people and feels their need. Jesus also felt compassion for a large crowd. Can you find an example of this in the
   Bible?

CHAPTER 20

1. Because of Kendrick's loyalty and faithfulness to the Prince, a
   haven is started in a city that only weeks earlier was in almost
   total rebellion to the King's good ways. All of this was accom-
   plished by the power of the Prince. The power of Christ
   doesn't change and is always available to those who seek it,
   yet our efforts for Him are not always so successful. What
   does this tell you about the importance of faithfulness and
   loyalty on our part?

2. We learned that each book in the Knights of Arrethtrae Series
   deals with a specific set of vices and virtues. Review the two
   vices and two virtues that are dealt with in *Sir Kendrick and
   the Castle of Bel Lione*. What are they? Which characters represented these traits?

3. Did any of the characters you identified in question 2 have a
   heart change in regard to their vices? If so, what do you think
   caused the change in each case? What circumstances developed
   the virtues in the characters you identified?

4. Have you realized anything new or thought about changing
   anything in your own life because of the tale of *Sir Kendrick
   and the Castle of Bel Lione*?

5. The theme verse for this book is Isaiah 42:6–7. What does this
   verse say about the power of Christ in people's lives?

ANSWERS TO DISCUSSION QUESTIONS

Review Questions from the Kingdom Series

1. The Prince represents Jesus Christ.
2. The Knights of the Prince represent all Christians.
3. The Noble Knights represent the Jewish religious leaders during the time of Christ (for example, the scribes, Pharisees, teachers of the Law, and so on).
4. Chessington represents Jerusalem, and Arrethtrae represents the whole world (the words *earth* and *terra* are combined backward to make up this word).
5. The Dark Knight, also referred to as Lucius, represents Satan.
6. The Silent Warriors are God's angels, and the Shadow Warriors are Satan's demons.
7. A haven represents a local church where believers are trained, discipled, and sent out to share the gospel with others.

Questions for *Sir Kendrick and the Castle of Bel Lione*

CHAPTER 1

1. Jesus deals with us in grace, while the world is geared toward evaluating others based on performance and works. The Bible teaches that a person can be instantly saved through faith in Christ. The training and discipleship come afterward.
2. One choice is 2 Corinthians 10:17–18; answers based on personal experience.
3. For example, "The church is a body of believers, not a building," or "I don't find my worth in trendy clothes but in my identity in Christ."
4. The Council of Knights represents the leadership of the early church and primarily the apostles.

5. When we have conflicts with other people, we must realize that the problem is not actually with those people but with the work the devil is trying to do in all of our lives. People often don't realize that their actions are sinful and in line with what Satan would want, especially if those people aren't saved. (Rest of answer based on personal experience.)

6. If we are living godly Christian lives, we will experience persecution, but we can welcome it without shame and with rejoicing because the spirit of glory and of God rests upon us. When the fullness of Christ's glory is revealed to us, we will be exceedingly joyful that God counted us worthy to share in even a little bit of Jesus' sufferings so that the gospel could be spread! See what Jesus had to say about persecution in John 15:18–20 and 16:33. Christians all over the world are experiencing different levels of persecution; an Internet search for "Christian persecution" will bring up several Christian Internet news sources.

7. Being aware of Satan's devices can help us live more victorious Christian lives by keeping us safe from the deception, confusion, and torment he can so craftily bring to unsuspecting and vulnerable people. Several things might happen if we dwell on the plans of the devil instead of focusing on the good plans of the Lord. First of all, we might begin to fear. Even though we know we have no reason to fear since "perfect love casts out fear" (1 John 4:18) and "He who is in you is greater than he who is in the world" (1 John 4:4), spending too much time investigating evil can sometimes affect our perspective. Second, we might unwittingly allow the devil to steal our joy—and the joy of the Lord is a precious and powerful thing that should be carefully guarded. Third, we might give the devil undue attention (which is really what he wants—to get the glory God deserves) and begin to see him as bigger and more powerful

than he really is. Fourth, our mission to share the good news can be thwarted by our spending too much time battling darkness. Though it is necessary to take time and effort to tear down strongholds, allowing more people to come to the knowledge of the truth, we must remember that the devil has already been defeated by Jesus. Finally, we might miss the precious guidance, direction, and quality time building our relationship with the Lord if we spend all of our time talking to and rebuking the devil. (Other responses possible.)

CHAPTER 2

1. Answer based on personal experience.
2. The tournaments bring to remembrance Kendrick's painful past. However, once he recognizes the intensity of evil in Sir Casimir, Kendrick realizes the depth of what he is facing and the importance of his mission for the Prince. This recognition brings a renewed willingness to do what is necessary to find the information that brought him to the tournament. This applies to us as believers because we need, as 1 Peter 5:8 tells us, to "Be sober, be vigilant; because [our] adversary the devil walks about like a roaring lion, seeking whom he may devour." We need to be able to see with clarity as Kendrick did and be willing to do what it takes to stand up to evil, even if it means doing something we dislike.
3. One possibility is 2 Corinthians 5:17.

CHAPTER 3

1. The word *evil* is contrasted with the word *single*. *The Message* paraphrases Matthew 6:22–23 like this: "Your eyes are windows into your body. If you open your eyes wide in wonder and belief, your body fills up with light. If you live squinty-eyed in

greed and distrust, your body is a dank cellar. If you pull the blinds on your windows, what a dark life you will have!" *Single* in this verse refers to having your focus and direction set on God and God alone—singularity of vision.

2. Read Romans 12:17–21. (Rest of answer based on personal experience.)

CHAPTER 4

1. Duncan wants to prove himself as a knight to Kendrick and the Council of Knights in order to get the respect he feels he deserves as a Knight of the Prince. He should be content with his identity in the Prince and know that his own achievements can do nothing to elevate himself any further than being considered worthy to be called a Knight of the Prince.

2. The giant man may be frustrated or perhaps even angry with Duncan for his impulsive behavior and for risking the mission by acting alone without counsel.

CHAPTER 5

1. A few choices include Mark 6:7 and Luke 10:1; Proverbs 12:15; 15:22; and 20:18; and also Genesis 25:29–34 and Hebrews 12:14–17.

2. Answer based on personal experience. Though it's not easy, the Bible clearly tells us that we must die to ourselves (Galatians 2:20) and present ourselves to God as living sacrifices (Romans 12:1). John the Baptist put it this way: "He must increase, but I must decrease" (John 3:30). Kendrick puts the mission of the Prince first. Since Duncan and Kendrick have obtained the information they needed, further participation is not only unnecessary but a waste of time and energy and a pointless risk of injury and discovery.

CHAPTER 6

1. Ra + Bel Lione = RaBelLione (rebellion). The vice or stronghold of rebellion is visible in the conversation between Brack and his friends, in the tavern when a father expected that his daughter would sneak out and attend the festival if he didn't allow her to go, in Hamlin's leaving in the middle of the night to join his friends at the festival, and in the fact that Hamlin and the youth of Bel Lione refuse to discuss the festivals with adults.

2. The festival represents the temptation to rebel against authority, and going to the festival represents rebelling. No one can attend just once because once a person tastes the "adventure" of choosing to sin, he or she finds it difficult to refuse in the future, especially if it is seen as acceptable in the culture. Consciously choosing to walk in darkness changes a person.

CHAPTER 7

1. When we focus on the Lord, our priorities fall into proper alignment. Not only do our relationships with others improve, but we also begin to see positive changes in our attitudes, reactions, choices, and our lives in general. When we make God our top priority, we become spiritually mature. See Matthew 6:33 and Ephesians 4:14–15.

CHAPTER 8

1. First, Duncan went alone. Second, he did not have his sword or his armor. The sword represents God's Word, which is our only offensive weapon in our battle against Satan (as described in Ephesians 6:10–17). Duncan was injured because he didn't have his full armor.

2. Answers based on personal experience. The best way to deal with temptation is the same way Jesus dealt with it—with the

sword of God's Word. Matthew 4:1–11 gives us an account of how Satan tempted Jesus in the wilderness and how Jesus quoted Scripture in every instance to defeat Satan. It is important for us to read God's Word and to memorize Scripture so we are ready to use it when the tempter comes our way. Also see James 4:7 and 1 Corinthians 10:13.

3. John 1:3 says Jesus (the Word) made everything, including all heavenly beings. Satan and his demons know the power of Christ and tremble, for they also know their future. Matthew 25:41 says that the everlasting fire is prepared for the devil and his angels. Christ's ultimate victory over Satan occurred at the cross and through His resurrection, when the works of Satan were destroyed. See James 2:19; 1 John 4:4; Romans 16:20; 2 Timothy 1:7–12; 1 John 3:8; Romans 8:37.

CHAPTER 9

1. Kendrick is not afraid because he has something great and powerful to draw upon. The resource he draws on is his identity as a Knight of the Prince, who confers His power and authority on those who follow Him. This represents the power and authority given to us by Jesus (see Matthew 16:19; Luke 10:19; 1 John 4:4; Romans 15:13; 1 Corinthians 1:23–25; and Revelation 12:11).

2. Isaiah 14:12–20 and Revelation 12:1–11.

3. Bronwyn is deeply affected by Lucius's insurrection since his best friend was won over by the darkness. Answers based on personal experience.

CHAPTER 10

1. People "play in the shadows of darkness" by choosing to participate in sinful activities as a result of peer pressure. For young

people, the "fun" but mischievous activities they participate in can often quickly lead to a stronghold that they may struggle with for the rest of their lives. Drinking alcohol, taking drugs, viewing inappropriate movies or images, and gambling are just a few examples of activities that can lead to life-destroying addictions.

2. This is dangerous because Satan is crafty and effective in using this attitude to capture people into living a lifestyle of sin. It is the hook that is not easily dislodged.

3. The stronghold of rebellion is manifested in the youth as they participate in getting drunk, showing inappropriate affection with each other, and reveling in violence.

CHAPTER 11

1. Kendrick's actions finally convinced Landor when words could not. He displayed mercy (by not striking Landor when he had the chance), vulnerability (by opening his arms and lowering his sword when he could have continued the duel), and trust (by removing his breastplate and allowing Landor to advance in spite of the obvious risk of attack) to demonstrate his intention of peace. Our witness as Christians is much more effective if we "walk the talk" and are courageous enough to befriend those who need Christ.

CHAPTER 12

1. Kendrick is speaking of the Prince (Jesus). One choice is John 6:28–58.

2. Answers based on personal experience.

3. Hypocrisy (Hypoc), lying (Deceptor), intoxication (Toxica), partying (Revel), self-indulgence (Plezior), pride (Arrogoy), destruction (Destroyer), death (Carnage), turmoil (Chaos),

and affliction (Tormentor). Rebellion breeds destructive behavior just as Lord Ra breeds the beasts. This behavior in turn guards the darkened heart from allowing the righteousness of the Lord to enter in, just as the beasts guard the walls of the castle to help secure this evil stronghold from good entering in and triumphing.

4. Jesus faithfully faced and overcame the obstacles of being tempted to sin, being completely separated from the Father for a time, and having to endure extreme suffering on the cross to pay for our salvation and triumph over evil. While all this was difficult and His humanity cried out against doing these things (see Mark 14:32–36), He was faithful to the end and loyal in accomplishing His mission.

CHAPTER 13

1. Second Timothy 1:7 is a good verse about overcoming fear. We don't have to be afraid because the Holy Spirit lives within us and is greater than "he who is in the world" (1 John 4:4)!

2. Satan uses many devices to try to hinder our work for the Lord. He can (and does!) use fear, mental distraction, sickness, procrastination, temptation, disagreements among believers, and a variety of other tools to hinder our work with the ultimate goal of terminating it.

CHAPTER 14

1. Answer based on personal experience. Jesus tells us that there are many lost people ready to be brought to salvation, but the workers in this spiritual harvest are few, so we should pray that God will send more workers. We should pray for ourselves as workers, too, so that by the Holy Spirit we'll be able to see the opportunities when God presents them.

CHAPTER 15

1. There are three roads a person can take once he decides to enter the stronghold of rebellion:

   A. The most common response is to get caught up in the indulgences and pleasures and to become discontented with the world outside of the rebellion. This will strain the person's relationship with authority figures. When this person grows up, he may leave the worst of the indulgences behind but still expect his own children to rebel against him. He may even consider this normal and healthy—not realizing how close he came to destruction and how he is allowing his children to do the same. Because sin is pleasurable for a time, he is blinded to the enduring goodness of walking in the light instead of the darkness. In our society, this response looks normal to many who expect rebellion from youth. Many teenagers happily dabble in illegal activities while their parents pretend not to know. Youth disrespect their parents by breaking or bending their rules, and parents wait in frustration for their children to grow up and become responsible. The effects of their rebellion may follow them as they continue to be discontent with a "boring and responsible" life and have trouble with authority figures like bosses, law-enforcement officers, the government, spouses, and even God.

   B. The second response is to become so taken with the sinful activities of rebellion that a person can think of nothing else. The person who responds this way eventually abandons everything in his former life (including things like relationships and future dreams) and chooses to live in complete darkness and sin. He becomes a prisoner of the devil, so weak and vulnerable to the power of the pleasure that he is unable ever to leave under his own power. The devil sets "snares of death" (Proverbs 14:27) for people in our society with drugs, alcohol, fornication, and other activities. However, the power of God can break these strongholds (2 Corinthians 10:4).

C. The third response is to grow strong from the rebellion rather than weak. This is most desirable to the powers of evil because these people can be used to spread and cultivate evil. These people are represented by the Vincero Knights. Some examples of who these people might be in our society include drug dealers, murderers, slave traders, and sex traffickers. The good news is, the transforming peace of Jesus' love can save even one such as this.

2. A fourth response would be to refuse to enter the stronghold of rebellion in the first place. Youth in our society make this response by respecting the authority of their parents and choosing to walk the path of righteousness. Ultimately, maintaining a good relationship with the Lord is the only thing that will protect us from the schemes of the devil. Elise is an example of a character who chose this response.

3. Two good choices are John 3:16 and 2 Peter 3:9.

CHAPTER 16

1. No one can fathom the richness of God's good plans, both here on earth—in Christ—and in heaven. Rest of answer based on personal experience.

2. Kendrick's call to battle symbolizes the need for Christians to unite in Christ in order to reach the lost and to stand against evil. We battle against evil not with worldly weapons but with the Word of God and the power of prayer in the authority of Jesus' name. Personal and corporate prayer is one of the most powerful and effective weapons to use against Satan.

Revival begins with God's people dedicating themselves to prayer. Acts 2:42–47 is an excellent example of the power of prayer, fellowship, and unity in the cause to further God's kingdom.

3. One choice is Gideon. In Judges 7–8 you can read the amazing story of how God used this meek servant and only 300 men to defeat an army of 135,000. God did and still does this so that no one will wonder whose power accomplishes the goal. If the vessel God uses is fully capable of succeeding on his own, God does not receive any glory. God loves to use unlikely candidates. This tactic builds great faith and blesses both the person (or people) and God!

4. Some possibilities are Ephesians 6:12; 2 Corinthians 10:3–5; Galatians 5:1; 1 John 4:4; Ephesians 6:11.

CHAPTER 17

1. Duncan made a "deliberate decision to embrace the pain, to let it make him stronger." Jesus says that we must deny ourselves and take up our cross and follow Him. Often this is not easy, for it may require us to face our fears and possibly even persecution as represented by the cross.

CHAPTER 18

1. One choice is Mark 9:23. (Rest of the answer based on personal experience.)

2. Second Corinthians 10:1–6.

3. The words of the Prince draw Kendrick to realize that he can forgive Landor. This symbolizes the importance of rooting God's Word deep in our hearts, because the Word will lead us down the right path. Forgiveness is so important because it is the very heart of God—"while we were yet sinners, Christ died for us" (Romans 5:8, KJV).

4. Kendrick's testimony for the Prince through his words and his life finally convinces Landor to believe in Him. We should live our lives as though every moment we are witnessing to others for Jesus (because we are!). Inviting someone to believe in the real Prince, Jesus Christ, and to receive salvation through Him is simple. Romans 10:9 says, "If you confess with your mouth the Lord Jesus and believe in your heart that God has raised Him from the dead, you will be saved." John 3:16 is also an excellent verse to help lead someone to Jesus.

CHAPTER 19

1. This is a reference to God's restraint put upon Satan and his demons until the end times as indicated in Revelation 9 and also in Luke 8:27–31, where Jesus could have cast the legion of demons into the abyss.
2. Kendrick's prison was revenge. Jesus sets us free from all types of "prisons," including grudges, greed, hatred, fear, religious legalism, addictions, and many more.
3. A similar story is the parable of the prodigal son, found in Luke 15:11–32.
4. One example is Mark 6:30–34.

CHAPTER 20

1. If Christians aren't determined to be faithful and loyal to Christ, believing His Word even when the world tries to convince us otherwise, we won't be able to access the mighty power He has made available to us. Just as Bronwyn had long been aching for something to be done and jumped at the chance to help the Knights of the Prince when Kendrick made the decision to stand up to evil, the Lord's power is ready and waiting to be used.

2. The chief vices are rebellion and impulsiveness (or foolishness), and the virtues are forgiveness and loyalty. Hamlin, the prisoners, the Vincero Knights, and many of the other citizens of Bel Lione represent the trait of rebellion. Duncan represents the trait of impulsiveness or foolishness. Ancel represents the traits of rebellion and foolishness. Elise and Lady Odette represent the trait of loyalty, and Kendrick represents the traits of loyalty and forgiveness.

3. Ancel's heart change was caused by the immediate consequences his choice brought. Many of the prisoners' hearts were changed by the realization that their behavior had caused their imprisonment. Landor was changed first by the recognition of extreme evil and then by the love and forgiveness that the Prince showed him through Kendrick. Duncan was changed by the suffering (including his own, Elise's, and Kendrick's) that was caused by his unwise and rash behavior. Forgiveness was developed in Kendrick because coming face to face with the object of his former fury tested his faith in the Prince and forced him to finally give up the pain of his past through forgiving this enemy that he loved. Loyalty was developed through his relationships with Duncan and Teara. The realization that no one else would rescue these people and the need to persevere in order to do it spurred him on.

4. Answer based on personal experience.

5. "I the LORD have called thee in righteousness, and will hold thine hand, and will keep thee, and give thee for a covenant of the people, for a light of the Gentiles; to open the blind eyes, to bring out the prisoners from the prison, and them that sit in darkness out of the prison house." (Isaiah 42:6–7, KJV)

Call to Courage

Written by Emily Elizabeth Black

AUTHOR COMMENTARY

Unlike the Kingdom Series allegory, in which characters and events are based on people and events taken directly from Scripture, the Knights of Arrethtrae Series presents biblical principles allegorically. Each book teaches about virtues and vices conveyed through the truth of God's Word. *Sir Kendrick and the Castle of Bel Lione* teaches about loyalty, forgiveness, foolishness, and rebellion.

Rebellion of the heart is always a dangerous path, for it is preceded by pride and always separates us from the Lord. Our culture today encourages it, not fully understanding the consequences of dancing about its flames. It seems to especially strike the heart of youth whose understanding and wisdom have not yet fully matured. It is my heart to honor the Lord by opening the eyes of some to the dreadful consequences of a rebellious heart and to the joyful reward of loyalty and forgiveness. But ultimately it is my prayer that all who read this allegory of biblical principles will be drawn to Jesus Christ and trust in Him as Lord and Savior.

For though we walk in the flesh, we do not war according to the flesh. For the weapons of our warfare are not carnal but mighty in God for pulling down strongholds.

—2 CORINTHIANS 10:3–4